THE HAMPTONS REAL ESTATE HORROR SHOW

ANONYMOUS TIMES TWO
ILLUSTRATED BY ANONYMOUS

iUniverse, Inc.
Bloomington

The Hamptons Real Estate Horror Show

iUniverse books may be ordered through booksellers or by contacting:

iUniverse
1663 Liberty Drive
Bloomington, IN 47403
www.iuniverse.com
1-800-Authors (1-800-288-4677)

ISBN: 978-1-4620-6421-2 (sc)
ISBN: 978-1-4620-6423-6 (hc)
ISBN: 978-1-4620-6422-9 (e)

Printed in the United States of America

iUniverse rev. date: 11/21/2011

If you add together the time we've spent in real estate, it comes to almost fifty years. So we know a thing or two; we've been around the block. Of course, we've met some nice people over the years, but they don't make for interesting stories.

Office Manager: You're being sued.

Me: I'm being sued?

Office Manager: Yes, you're being sued; therefore, the agency is being sued.

Me: Who's suing me?

Office Manager: The Graves. They say that the house you rented them wasn't clean.

Me: Wasn't clean? Why didn't they call me? I could have dealt with it!

Office Manager: I guess they'd rather sue you.

QUALITY COUNTS

She was referred to me by a broker in New York City. While I always try to do the best job I can for a customer, referrals hold even more significance, since it's not only my reputation on the line, but also that of the person who referred me.

She's a professional renter. She and her family have been renting for years and will only look at houses in those areas from which they can walk to the particular beaches they prefer. She has provided me with a list of prerequisites before coming out to look, which helped in selecting the houses to show her but made for only a handful of choices.

"I'll take my car, and you take yours," is the first thing she says in response to my "hello" as she walks into our office. "I'll follow you."

Okay, I think, *we're all business—cut out the niceties.* After all these years in the business, I know the streets, and I know the houses, but when someone is following me, I'll more than likely mess up. I go by the street or pass the driveway, and I have to repeatedly back up or U-turn, making me feel foolish—and extremely aware that the customer concurs. This makes me even more nervous. So after a couple of U-turns and a backup or two, we arrive at the first house.

She examines it carefully—very, very carefully, inch by inch, pot by pot, bed by bed—and declares it perfect. However, she still wants to see the others on my list, in case there's something better than perfect. After looking at the three other contenders, she proclaims the first one the winner, tells me to send her a lease, and drives off.

The months pass, and it's finally Thursday, the day before the Memorial Day weekend. I leave my house at seven in the morning to check on all the houses I've rented, making sure everything is in order. I've learned from experience that most of the owners schedule the cleaning people to come in that last day, so going any earlier is usually a waste of time. I check the house she's rented and find it perfectly clean and ready. Then I call her and tell her where I've hidden the key, since she and her family will be arriving the next evening after office hours.

At the end of the day on Friday, with my tenants ensconced in their houses, I leave the office and go home to greet my weekend guests. The grill is fired up and I have taken my first swallow of a margarita when the phone rings.

"You must come over here immediately!" It's her.

"What's the trouble? Didn't you find the key?"

"I found the key; I'm in the house. You *must* come here immediately!"

"I checked the house today, and everything looked to be in perfect order. Please tell me what's the matter."

"I can't discuss it on the phone. Come right now—it's urgent!" She slams the phone down.

My friends try to urge me to stay home. The hell with her, they say; office hours are over, and this is your holiday, too. As much as I agree with them, I feel obliged to go, so I plunge myself into the horrendous traffic. After covering a distance that would normally take me twenty minutes, I arrive at the house an hour and ten minutes later.

"At last!" are her words of welcome, with no effort to conceal her annoyance. "Come with me," she commands as she starts up the stairs. She enters the master bathroom, yanks open the linen closet, and pulls out a white towel. "Feel this towel!" she says, thrusting the offensive item toward me. "I want you to feel the quality of this towel. Would you dry your face on this?"

"Oh, by the way, I have three dogs and three little boys, but they're all very well behaved. Actually, the dogs are better behaved than the kids. I have certificates from the obedience school I can show the landlord. Wish I had them for the boys."

TAKING IT ALL IN STRIDE

A week in a hectic season goes something like this:

A fashion photographer makes an appointment to see a large contemporary on a large lot with a separate large barn. I arrive early to wait for him. I see his MG approach, the top down, with what appears to be several people jammed inside. He careens into the drive and comes to a dangerous stop just inches from where I am standing.

After he gets out, three young women unfold themselves from the backseat of the car. Each girl is well over six feet tall; lined up end to end with their arms outstretched, they would reach from one end of the lot to the other. Together they can weigh no more than a hundred pounds. They are standing very close together—probably, I reason, because individually, they would risk transparency. The man introduces them, and of course they speak no English. One of them, the tallest, whom I've seen on the cover of *Vogue*, has a small growth on her midsection—an abnormality that turns out to be an eight-and-a-half-month pregnancy. Each of them is tanned to a fare-thee-well and wears a little piece of gauze, a sarong of sorts, over an itsy-bitsy bikini. They have all just come from the beach.

"They'll wait," the photographer says as we walk toward the entrance to the house and they drape themselves very tightly together over and around the split-rail fence. Seen from a distance, arms in the air and feet turned out in a collective plié, they look like a flower arrangement, or an exotic vine growing up the fence.

The house won't do, and the barn looks too new, so they all drive off after the man calls the women together like a border collie running a small and prize-winning herd. I watch as they climb—moving as one again—into the back of his small car. They smile and wave as they speed off to buy a leaf of lettuce for dinner and a six-pack of Perrier.

Later that same week, a colleague is referred to a rising film star. We all know his name and reputation. He needs to buy a house immediately, but it won't be easy, since he's been on drugs since the age of fifteen and forgets whatever happens immediately after the fact.

My colleague takes the star's agent to see a house she thinks might work; she can't believe her good fortune when he tells her his client will take it. Inside the house, the owner, an aging ex-beauty, is supine on her couch. Not able or not bothering to get up, she tells the star's agent the house is in mint condition; no inspection will be needed.

"He'll take it—there's no time for an inspection anyway. It'll do."

Two days later, at 6:00 a.m., a man shows up at the house. He is wearing blue bell-bottoms, flip-flops, an enormous red-and-yellow-checkered hat, and aviator glasses. The owner of the house, the aging beauty, answers the door.

"I'm here to see the house," the man says, with no apparent concern for the time. "My agent tells me I bought it." Frantic at the sight of him and wondering whether he might be mad, the woman rushes to call my colleague, insisting she come over immediately. It is 6:15 a.m.

When my colleague arrives, she finds the film star and the aging beauty sitting on the deck, trading pasts, drinking Bloody Marys. The sun is just coming up, and the deal is as good as done.

After a couple from Manhattan has viewed ten houses for sale (one of which they swooned over and stayed in for over an hour), they get in their car and head back to the city. Somewhere between Manorville and Manhattan, they call me.

"Now that you know what we like," they say, "we know you'll call us when you find it."

IT'S IN THE STARS

"I saw your sign on a piece of land in that Napeague area. How much is it?" the woman on the other end of the phone whispers.

"Actually, there are three separate pieces, each one a third of an acre." I give her the prices.

"Okay" she whispers. "Could I get a discount if I buy all three?"

"I'll have to discuss that with the owner," I whisper back. "Are you prepared to make an offer?"

"Look," she says, her voice barely audible, "I got three children, and they're all about to graduate—one from college and two from high school. I wanna give them this land as graduation presents, but I gotta buy it right away. We gotta hurry—we gotta do this by the end of the day tomorrow. You understand?"

"Yes, I understand," I whisper conspiratorially, trying to understand. I explain, "The owner of the land lives in California, meaning that since it's nine o'clock here, it's only six o'clock in the morning there, so I'll have to wait a little while before calling him." She seems to grasp the problem and gives me her number at work.

"When you call me, though, don't mention anything about why you're calling. If I can't come to the phone, just leave your name, not your number, and I'll call you back. Remember, don't leave me any messages."

An hour later, she's whispering into the phone again. "What did he say?"

"I haven't called him yet; it's still too early."

"You gotta hurry, I'm telling you! Call me!" She hangs up.

About twenty minutes later, she calls again. "What did he say, this man? What did he say about the price for all three pieces?"

"I still haven't called him. It's only seven twenty in the morning out there. I've got to wait a little longer."

She gives me her number at home. "Honey," she whispers, this time a little panicky, "if you don't have an answer until tonight, and you call me at home, and my husband answers and asks why you want to talk to me, don't tell him. If he asks who you are, you tell him your name, and that's all. If he asks what company you're with, don't tell him. If he asks if it's anything to do with land, just laugh and change the subject. But get back to me right away. I must buy by tomorrow. The stars are in the right place. You understand, right?"

Right.

I'm showing a house for the third time to the same couple. It's an overcast day, and although the house would look a lot brighter if I could pull up the Venetian blinds, the owner has insisted that I only turn the rod that will open the blinds to a horizontal position, and that I should not, under any circumstances, pull them up. So I obey the request, strange as it is.

I'm in the kitchen with the wife, and the husband is in one of the bedrooms. They love it and say they're going to call me the next day with an offer. I walk around, turning off the lights, and see that the husband has pulled up one of the blinds.

I quickly close it and call the owner in New York to tell her that she's going to have an offer the next day.

"DON'T PULL UP THE BLINDS!" is the first thing she shouts. "I told you that you may open them, but you are never to pull them up! Do you hear me?"

What was with those blinds? What was with the owner?

YOU NEVER KNOW WHO'S CALLING

Another Sunday, and the phone isn't ringing. No one drops by to look for a house to buy or rent. We're in the recession of 2008, and the money has either dried up or is in hiding.

Late Sunday morning, out of the blue, the phone finally rings. The secretary tells Dorothy there's a customer on the line. "You have an *up*" she screams.

"Hello?" Dorothy says calmly and coolly, as if the phone has been ringing all along, and she and our office are immune to the drought that has affected *all* the money in the country, "May I help you?"

The man on the other end of the line is calling about the $30 million property on the ocean in Southampton. It's Dorothy's listing, and she's advertising it, even though she counseled the sellers that this is not the best time to sell. They, however, insisted.

"It only takes one buyer," they said.

The man on the phone is on his way to South America, he tells her, but will come out next week before he leaves. He tells her he travels with one other person and three guard dogs. Dorothy is told to expect him on Friday.

"You see?" Dorothy says. "It was the ad. I *knew* I'd get a response. I bet you this guy buys it."

Fat chance, we all think, in this new environment of cutting back that has arrived overnight.

But the ad is great, we all agree. It features a huge color photo of the house and the manicured green lawn leading down to the ocean. The photos were taken on a perfect cloudless day. When you look at the photo, it makes you think that if you lived there, anything would be possible—anything. Dorothy and her sellers were sure that if any money remained in the country (or anywhere in the world), this mouthwatering ad would bring it out.

And, seemingly, it has. Dorothy asks for his name and address, and we spend the next hour huddled around her desk, as she runs an Internet search for his place of residence. First we bring up his state, Florida. Here is the overview: Florida as seen from way out in space. Then we home in, closer and closer, until finally we see a long driveway and then a very high and elaborate gate. We are so close that now we can read the plaque beside the gate.

And there it is, clear as crystal: Gainesville State Prison.

Looking closer, we see the razored and electrified fence. We spot some dogs in the distance—probably the dogs he referred to in his call.

Once Dorothy finally calms down, she wonders how "this felon, this *fake*, for God's sake" saw the ad. "How would he get hold of a copy of *"Homes & Land"*?" Sarcastically, she asks, "Does our distribution include prisons?"

We look at one another.

Well, why not? What better place to distribute our listings than to prisons? After all, sooner or later, the most famous and notorious CEOs will get out, and they'll need a place to live.

Dorothy clears her desk, puts on her coat, and heads for home.

"Hi, I'm calling from the real-estate agency to see if you have rented your house yet for August."

"No, I haven't. Your office is in the village, right?"

"Yes, it is. Why?"

"Would you do me a favor? Would you go to Citarella and get me a half-pound of flounder?"

LOVE LETTERS

Broker to Landlord: November 16

"Your tenants from this summer are wondering when they'll get their security deposit back, minus whatever deductions, which must be accompanied by copies of the bills. According to the lease, the deposit is to be returned within forty-five days, and it's now been sixty-two days."

Landlord to Broker: November 17

"I am working to provide a response. I'm in Ecuador, and there have been terrible landslides here, plus the mail system is awful."

Tenant to Broker: January 24

"I'm still waiting for the return of my security deposit. He's now ninety days late. I think we've allowed sufficient time for the landlord to deal with the floods, landslides, and earthquakes he claims beset him, to return the deposit."

Tenant to Landlord: January 28

"You are now three months behind on returning the security deposit of $1,000. As I understand from the lease, the deposit should have been returned by forty-five days after the end of our lease. Please send me the check immediately."

Landlord to Tenant: January 31

"Here are the charges I have so far for the cable, electric, heat, and water. There will be additional charges to have the bedding and sofa slipcover professionally laundered and to have pet waste removed from the lawn."

Tenant to Landlord: January 31

"First of all, we already paid the cable bill. As for the oil, there is no way we could have used a whole tank of heating oil in a week. The tank was empty. As for the bedding, we had it professionally cleaned before we left the house. The sofa cover was a mess when we got there—so much so that we moved it into another room, so we wouldn't have to sit on it. I'm not going to pay for this to be cleaned. The lawn was spotless when we left; we planted flowers and cleaned debris such as beer cans from the front and back lawns, and if there was pet waste, it could only have happened after we left, since our dog did his business at the end of the street and we always cleaned it up. We bought you lawn furniture, because yours was in terrible shape . We went the first two weekends with no means of cooking, and in addition, the house had a terrible odor. It seems to me you don't give a damn for the contract, and you are seriously beginning to irritate me. I am asking you to rise to the occasion and be grateful for how much we spent on cleaning up your house and the improved condition we left it in. Pay us by the end of this week, and we can all move on."

Landlord to Tenant: January 31

"Stop being a shrew. I really could give a shit. I have many rental properties and could care less about $1,000. Stop acting like an asshole. Sue me. And go fuck yourself."

"My wife was awakened at five-thirty this morning by the birds!"
"Oh, I'm so sorry to hear that, but what would you like me to do?"
"Have them eliminated!"

SECOND SIGHT

I was sitting in the downstairs office, up against the large picture window that faced the street. It was the early eighties; we were a small, privately owned real-estate agency and one of only a handful. The secretary told me I had a call.

"This is Tim Holden," the man said. "I work in the advertising office across the street from you. Look over, and you'll see me."

I looked and there was a man, on the phone, and he was waving.

"I work in advertising," he said, "but I also can *see* things." He explained, "I have premonitions. I can see things that are about to happen. I've done readings for some important people out here—Hollywood people and Wall Street guys. I have something to tell you … something I've seen for you."

I was just starting out in this new profession. I had no real idea of what was involved. But it seemed to me reading one's palm, or seeing into the future, was as reliable as anything I'd picked up in real-estate school.

"You're going to get a call from a man who wants to come out this coming Friday"—this was Tuesday—"to look at a house your agency has for sale on the ocean. He will end up buying it and you'll be the person who helps make this deal."

Back then, in the early eighties, there were only about five houses for sale on the ocean, and nothing was listed for more than $3 million. Three million dollars, however, was more than my father had earned in his first five years in business. It was more than our two houses and combined ten acres cost—more than all our cars and college educations cost. With the money from this deal, I could buy the moon.

"He's going to come on Friday ," Tim continued. "You'll meet him at a house on Gin Lane."

A half an hour later, the call came. I got the prospective buyer's name, made the appointment for Friday, and ran upstairs to the office of the manager (who was cordoned off from the rest of us, like the Wizard of Oz, and was just as mysterious) to tell him.

He smiled a wizardly smile and said nothing but "Good luck." But later I found out he had checked the man's name and financials and found this call was authentic. When, after the Friday showing, I came back to the office to report, he informed me that if there were a second call or showing, he'd come along.

And he did. That next time around, I was in Vanna White mode, dressed up as a real-estate salesperson. I tagged along and watched as my manager talked about the property, but generally said very little. The two men got along well. I was treated with courtesy but was clearly not essential to this very complicated and important deal.

No matter. The negotiations began. They went on for weeks and months. After a price was finally agreed upon, I became a gofer. I opened the house to let the architects and the appraiser in; I did comparables; I was there to let the inspectors in; and when the new owner's decorator came by to take measurements, I followed him around and held the measuring tape.

These chores took place over the summer. Every day was, because of that house, perfect. An endless blue sky presided over perfectly warm days. The ocean was just a few feet away, off the veranda.

I took the house, and my responsibility toward it and its new owner, very seriously. I *loved* this house. I loved its beautiful rooms, circa the early 1900s, I loved its windows overlooking the sea and its grand dining room, with space enough for twenty. I loved its wood-paneled living room, the kitchen, and the butler's pantry. I imagined a gracious lifestyle reminiscent of days gone by, and I was happy when its new owner claimed he hardly wanted to change it.

Time dragged on. My savings dwindled. I asked my manager when it might close. He wasn't sure. I asked the prophet from the building across the street who had seen this windfall in my future, when it was due to close. But he saw no date in his crystal ball.

"But it will close, won't it? I mean … you're sure of that, aren't you?"

"I saw it, so it's so," he said. My colleagues (equally as novice as me) were excited for me, with all of us coming to attention every time my phone rang.

And then, one day, the wizard-manager walked in and handed me an envelope. The house had closed. Eight months had passed since the buyer had first seen the house. I had a check, made out to me, for more money than I had ever seen. It was more than enough to pay my mounting debts, allow me to take a trip, and still put money in the bank. My colleagues took a photograph of me holding the check. My father was astounded and relieved, since he had subsidized me for years in my earlier so-called career in public relations.

I thanked my soothsayer friend in the building across the street. I thanked the wizard. I thanked the buyer. I thanked my lucky stars.

For a year or more, I was the richest and luckiest girl in town. I had been imprinted, right out of the gate, with the belief that such luck, even without my supposed prophet, could happen at any time, any moment, any day.

I continue to drive by the house on the ocean and to look up at the window of the building across the street from the office. The house, true to the buyer's word, has not been changed, but the man who foretold my future has left town.

"Is there anything else I should look for? Any sign? Anything else you see?" I asked before he left for a different life in Maine.

"I don't see things anymore," he said, as if choosing to leave the area had robbed him of his special sight.

"But you'll let me know, won't you? If you do see something, you'll let me know, won't you, please?"

"I don't do that anymore," he repeated, as if it were something about which he had a choice: he was leaving the area, and with it, the ability to see ahead.

Maybe he could only see things within a certain radius, I thought: his sight might be limited to the area in which he lived. Being that he might be a sort of GPS prophet, I was extremely lucky back then to have been the closest thing in sight.

"This is a very nice house," she says.
"I thought you'd like it," I agree.
"Let's see the kitchen," she says.
"Come with me," I reply. "It's over here."
"No VIKING RANGE? Forget it!" she shouts.
"But honey, you don't cook," he reasons.

ONE MORE FOR THE ROAD

The man on the phone tells me what kind of a house he is looking for and that he wants to come out the following morning to start his search. This is 1980, I have been in the business only about seven months, and this is a pretty impressive price range. I make appointments, collect the keys, and dash out to revisit some of the places to make sure they address his needs. By the end of the day, I have eliminated some houses and added others, and I am prepared for my appointment.

I arrive at the office really early the next morning to recheck my listings and make sure I haven't forgotten anything. I haven't been able to sleep anyway, nor have I been able to eat; not having worked in this elevated price range before, I am way too nervous for those sorts of activities.

At precisely nine o'clock, my customer arrives, a nice-looking man of about forty.

"Let's go," he says. "My car's out front."

"I'm ready," I reply. "My car's in the back."

"I'd rather we took mine, if you don't mind." We walk out the front door, and there at the curb is a very long, very black, very shiny limousine.

The chauffeur jumps out and holds the door open for Dr. Bliss and me.

"This is my driver, Matthew; this is my friend, Robert; and you can call me Justin," he says as we enter the padded leather interior. "You have to be in charge of giving directions to Matthew, though. Want a glass of champagne?" He pops the cork, takes out three crystal flutes from their built-in wooden cabinet, and starts pouring.

"I'll have to say no to that," I manage, "but thank you."

Robert and Justin first toast each other and then me. "Here's to our broker: she's going to find us the perfect house today."

This is a first, I think to myself. *Very amicable, very jolly.*

"Where we going?" Matthew calls from the front.

"Oh, sorry," I say, and I give him directions.

I show them all the houses on the list; they don't like any of them.

"Tell you what," Justin says, "it's lunchtime. How about we go out to Montauk for some lobsters? Will you join us? And afterward, we'll look at more expensive houses."

"Thanks so much, but if we're doing that, I'd better make some arrangements. I'll see you when you get back."

More expensive? This is amazing! I rush to my desk and begin flipping through the book of listings.

They come back at two o'clock, as arranged, and as I get into the limousine, Justin calls to Matthew, "First stop: wine shop. We're out of champagne!"

As Robert pops the cork, Justin holds out a glass to me. "You refused champagne before, and then you refused a lobster lunch. I'll be insulted if you don't join us now."

"Sure," I say. "Why not?" *Lobster,* I think. *I'd die for a lobster. Actually, I'd die for any kind of food, I'm starving!* I have just realized that it's two o'clock in the afternoon and I haven't eaten anything since lunch yesterday. That champagne tastes mighty fine.

As we drive along, they keep refilling my glass and theirs; I forget to give Matthew directions, we laugh a lot, and they like this second set of houses *much* better. We end up in the Northwest Woods section of East Hampton at sunset, and as we pull into the driveway of a very modern house, they open the fourth bottle of champagne.

"Thish looks really, really nish," Justin slurs. "Doeshn't it, Robert? Doeshn't it, Matthew? Doeshn't it look like a really nish housh? Doesh anybody live here?"

"No," I answer, "itsh shtill being built, but itsh allmosht finished."

"Okay," Justin says, "then we'll take our drinksh in with ush." I lead them to the front door, glass in one hand, batch of keys in the other, and finally manage to open the lock after a good deal of fumbling.

"Oh, thish ish *wonderful!*" they exclaim in unison.

"Jusht a minute, be right back," Justin says as he turns around and staggers to the car. He comes back with the bottle and another champagne glass. "Here, Matthew. I'm sho shorry. I wush leaving you out—we can't leave you out!" Justin pours his driver a drink. Matthew downs it. He refills the glass.

We find a radio sitting in the middle of the living-room floor, blasting out music at full volume. The contractor has obviously left it there for the next day.

"Ish there a pool?" Matthew asks, his chauffeur's cap askew.

"Sure," I answer, "itsh right out there"—I point to the glass sliding doors—"and theresh lotsh and lotsha decking, too! Go take a look."

They go outside to inspect it, and as the final rays of sunlight shine into the living room out of a glorious crimson sky, I begin dancing around the room to the music, champagne glass in one hand, my arms outstretched, my eyes closed.

"Buy thish housh, buy thish housh, why don'tcha? Buy thish housh, buy thish housh, oh won'tcha?" I sing, whirling, twirling, sipping, spilling. I'm loving real estate.

It is pitch black when we stumble out of there and into the car. "Where to?" Matthew asks, hiccupping.

"I guesh we're done for the day," Justin answers. "You'd better tell Matthew how to get out of here and back to your offish." I find that enormously amusing. I struggle enough to navigate this confusing new section of town in daylight, let alone in the dark and inebriated.

Somehow, I get us back to the office.

"You musht join us for a nish dinner before we go back home," Robert says. "Ishn't that right?"

"Thash right!" Justin and Matthew concur.

"Oh, I can't," I say. "I'm supposed to be meeting friends at a gallery opening right thish minute! But you shouldn't drive back to New York tonight. You should get yourshelvshs a hotel and drive in the morning."

When Justin calls the next morning, my head is throbbing. "We took your advice and stayed over last night in Southampton. Good thing we did; we couldn't have driven back. Matthew was smashed. Listen, I really like that house. I'd like to make an appointment to come back and look at it again. I'd also like to see what I can get if I up the ante."

Two weeks later, Justin and entourage return to look at the house again. He still loves it. He looks at even more expensive houses and loves them, too.

"When I buy a house," he says, "you'll have to come over and have dinner with us. I'm a great cook. And listen, do you ever get into

New York? I'm having a big party on the fifth, and I'd love it if you'd come—you'll have fun!"

"Thank you, Justin. I'd love to come."

"Great! I'll send you an invitation." And those words were the last I ever heard from him.

A woman comes into the office asking to see houses "south of the highway." Her budget isn't large enough to fund what she wants, and knowing this, I try to persuade her to look north of the highway, where she can get a lot more for the money.

"I *must* be south of the highway," she insists. When we get into the car and start out, she turns to me and asks, "What does 'south of the highway' mean, anyway?"

"DRAWING DEAD"

Two lawyers sit at the long table, along with a person from the title company, a bank attorney, and me. I am there to collect the commission at closing.

No one's talking, even though everyone seems to know one another. Papers go back and forth, people call out figures, and checks get signed. This goes on for about half an hour until suddenly the two lawyers begin whispering to one another.

"We were told the furniture was included," the buyer's lawyer says in a loud voice.

"No one ever told my client that," the seller's attorney says, "and he would never agree to that."

"Was the furniture in the living room when the walk-through took place?" The lawyer looks around the room while the question hangs in the air. Silence. The buyer's attorney asks where the broker is—and *who* the broker is.

I am sitting in a corner, trying to keep out of the way. I raise my hand.

"You did the walk-through for my client yesterday afternoon?"

"Yes." I tell him I called his client to say everything looked fine: the roof wasn't leaking, the doors and windows were intact, and the house was, as real-estate agents say, broom clean.

"Was the furniture in the living room?"

"Yes."

"Did you tell him that the furniture was there?"

"No, he didn't ask. I assumed the movers were coming later that day to pick it up ..."

"Never assume, Miss ... Miss? What is your name?" I am beginning to feel very odd. This is the first time anyone has mentioned the furniture—or me.

The two lawyers whisper together and then leave the room. Ten long minutes go by as we sit in silence. Another ten minutes. Everyone looks down at their papers, shuffles them, takes notes.

I should have brought a book, I think. I feel as if something bad is about to happen, like the feeling I have when a police car is behind me. My hands are beginning to sweat. *I just want to get out of here and go home.*

The door opens. The seller's attorney looks in, looks around the room.

"Miss ... Miss ..." And then he spots me. "Could you come out here a minute, please?"

What is going on? Whatever it is, it doesn't feel good. I try to tell myself to look nonchalant, casual, and confident, even though I suspect everyone here knows I've never been to a closing before.

"We have a problem here. Seems my client promised the buyer"— my customer—"according to his lawyer, that he'd include the living-room furniture in the sale. Were you told to put that into the original terms of sale?"

"No." I think back through all the steps, all the hundreds of phone calls before the buyer and seller reached an agreement. No, I would have remembered furniture. I am forever rearranging my own furniture.. I put great store by how a room looks. "No," I say again. "It was never mentioned."

The two men look at one another. "Well, it seems we're not going to be able to close today," the seller's attorney says.

I panic. My manager is expecting me back with a check. This is the first sale on my own. My half of the commission will make it possible for me to pay the bills that accumulated over the last eight months while I was learning the business and going into debt.

No one says anything. The three of us stand together in the middle of a huge room, which is empty except for one small table. On the table are a small lamp and a vase of ugly artificial flowers. *Here's a room that could really use the furniture ...*

"We've been trying to work this out," the buyer's attorney finally says. "Mr. Jones is willing to walk away unless he gets the furniture he was promised. Or said he was promised." *Who promised it?* I wonder.

"And Mr. Smith," the seller's attorney says, "isn't including the furniture and is perfectly willing to forget the deal. So you can see our dilemma. You can see the situation."

Actually, I can't. So I just stand there. I look around. This room would look really good if it had some comfortable upholstered chairs around a coffee table, some standing lamps, and real flowers on the table. At least then we could all sit down. The two men seem very relaxed, though I am hot and flushed and by now could really use a bathroom.

"Look, miss ..."—still, I am nameless—"We're all here prepared to close, to wrap up this deal. I'm sure you'd like to see that happen."

"Well, of course," I say.

"Good," they say in unison. "We knew you'd understand the situation," one continued. "We have to throw in the furniture. Mr. Smith is unwilling to include it, and Mr. Jones insists on it. However, Mr. Smith says he'll sell it at a considerable discount to get the deal done. $5,000 would do it. It's worth over $8,000 for everything, but in order to get on with this, he'll accept $5,000."

Still, I don't get it.

"Okay, fine," I say. Great. "What do I have to do with this?"

"Well, miss, the only way we can salvage this is if you agree to cut your commission."

An hour later, I'm back at the office with a check in hand—not for $15,000, but $10,000.

My manager looks at the check, looks at me, and asks what happened to the other $5,000.

He is clearly not happy when I tell him. "You should have called," he says. "You should have called their bluff and walked away." What is he talking about? If I'd done that, I wouldn't have even had this check!

"Since you let them do this, you are now in the unfortunate position of having to forfeit a part of your commission to make up for the agency's loss. Instead of the $7,500 you would have gotten, you'll be getting a check for $2,500. They tricked you. Let this be a lesson."

$2,500 won't pay my bills! I'm frantic, humiliated. Back at my desk, I burst into tears. A senior broker asks what's wrong, so I tell him the story.

"Honey," he says when I've finished my sad story, " you have to learn to play poker. You have to learn to bluff and *never, ever* fold. Real estate isn't really real estate; it's poker. This isn't really East Hampton; it's Las Vegas, and your closing was actually a poker game ... where *you* were drawing dead. "Learn to play poker. If you do, you'll know everything you need to know about real estate in the Hamptons."

"I don't know if you realize this, but your chaise lounges around the pool are very rickety and unstable. I'm afraid that if the tenants sit on them, the chairs may collapse, and someone might get hurt."

"Tell them not to use them."

This directive from the landlord who got $80,000 for a month's rental.

WESLEY AND AMANDA

"The house that was advertised in the *New York Times*? The one in Sagaponack for $6.8 million? We'd like to see that one, and we want to see it now."

"Okay," I say. (*Achtung!* I think) "Let me call the owners. While we're at it, perhaps you can tell me what you're looking for, just so I'll know."

"No, we have no time—we just want to see this one."

"The owner says it's fine to show the house," I tell her when I call back. "They're on their way out and will leave the door unlocked. How about if we meet at the Sagaponack General Store in fifteen minutes?"

"We're driving a silver BMW ... and I must tell you that, unfortunately, our mother's helper couldn't come out with us this weekend, so we'll be with our son. He's four years old. I hope you don't mind."

"Of course I don't mind! That's fine."

"Well, then, we're leaving now." She hangs up.

I pull up in front of the store, and I wait ... and I wait some more. Thirty-five minutes later, a silver BMW drives up next to me.

"Hi!" says the woman behind the wheel, who looks to be in her late twenties. "I'm Susan, and this is my husband, Daryl." Two children peered out of the backseat, a boy and a girl. "Let's go!" she calls out. "We have to get this done before nap time." The couple get out of their car and into mine, putting the children on their laps, saying, "This is Wesley, and this is Amanda."

I wonder who Amanda is, since they only mentioned that they were bringing their son. She seems to be about six years old, but when I hear the conversation between the two children, I decide that she must be Wesley's wife.

As I pull in the driveway, Susan asks, "Is this the house?"

"This is it."

"Oh, this is beautiful! Isn't it, Daryl?"

Daryl agrees.

"Look at the lawn!" Susan continues. "And I love the way the house sits back on the property! I love the way the driveway winds around!" We get out of the car. "Look at the landscaping, Daryl. Isn't it beautiful?" Daryl agrees. We go inside.

"Oh, look at the living room!" Susan gushes. "Look at that fireplace! This is great! Look at the kitchen! A big eat-in kitchen, just what we wanted! This is perfect!"

Wesley and Amanda open the door leading to the large backyard and pool area. Susan and Daryl continue to examine the appliances and cabinetry.

A few minutes later, when we are in the den, Wesley comes into the room, walks over to me, puts his hands on his hips, looks up at me, and asks defiantly, "Is that pool heated?"

I look down at this small child, who is no more than three feet tall, and assure him that yes, the pool is heated.

"Well," he challenges, "it sure doesn't *feel* heated." I explain that most likely, the heater was turned off. I can tell he doesn't believe me.

We all climb the wide staircase to the large landing on the second floor. There's a bedroom off each corner of the landing, and every bedroom has its own bath. The rooms are spacious and sunny, and the views from each are lovely, looking out at the manicured lawn and gardens. The master bedroom has a separate sitting area with a fireplace.

Wesley and Amanda run ahead of us, checking out the bedrooms, while Susan and Daryl linger over every detail. They're enchanted.

"This is perfect!" Susan says. "The bedrooms are so large without being overwhelming or cold; the proportions are wonderful."

"I love it!" Daryl agrees. "A fireplace in the master bedroom—how cool is that?"

We're back on the landing when Wesley and Amanda join us. Amanda looks at Susan and Daryl, her arms folded in front of her waist, her skinny little legs protruding from her checked shorts like two parallel twigs.

"Well, *I don't like it!*" she pronounces.

"You don't like it?" they echo. "Why don't you like it?"

"The bedrooms are too small."

"Oh, well." They turn to me. "That does it. The bedrooms are too small. Sorry."

"Let's go," Wesley says.

"Let's go," they agree.

"Do you have lights?"

"Who is this?"

"It's Vivian Ordener. Do you have lights?"

"I have no idea—I was sound asleep. Why are you calling me at this hour? What time is it?"

"It's eleven forty-five. I have no lights."

"It must be a blackout; that happens sometimes when it's been very hot and humid."

"Find out what's going on, and call me right back!"

When I called back, I explained, "I spoke with someone at the electric company, and it is a blackout. They're working on it. Just go to sleep; it will be fixed soon."

"If anything in my freezer spoils, there'll be hell to pay! I paid for a house with electricity!"

SECURITY MONEY

"When can I expect my security deposit back?" I can hear an edge to her voice. She is ready for a fight.

"Within forty-five days. The landlord is inspecting the house, and if anything needs repair, she'll need to get estimates."

"Like what?" I can hear from her tone that she is in her corner, ready for the bell, waiting for the fight to begin.

"Well, since you ask," I say, "I was at the house yesterday, and the owner pointed out a couple of things ..."

She is quiet. We wait one another out.

"Like what?" she asks finally, exasperated. She has taken off her robe and is pawing the ground.

"Well, like the dining-room chairs."

"What about them? We *had* to sit on them. She had plastic covers on them when we arrived. We couldn't very well sit on plastic covers—now could we?"

Her nasty "now could we" implied that I wouldn't know the difference between upholstery and plastic.

"No, but every one of the ten chairs is dirty and will have to be cleaned."

"I don't see why," she says. "It was normal wear and tear."

"Then there's the stain on the wooden floor," I say. "Yellow. Something yellow. Like paint ... or *urine*. Yes, like urine. Floor finishers will probably have to take a look."

No word from her end.

Another standoff ensues, so after a few minutes, I feel compelled to jump in.

"Also, the large stain in the back bedroom. On the carpet."

"We had all the carpets cleaned before we left," she says. "I can't imagine what you're referring to. It must have been there when we took occupancy."

"Well, no, it wasn't, because, you see, I inspected the house before you moved in and noted anything that might be wrong. The stain wasn't there."

"Normal wear and tear," she says again. It's beginning to sound like a country-and-western song. "We left that house in immaculate shape." I can hear that she feels there is nothing more to say and is about to hang up.

"Then there was the blue bowl," I say quickly. "It's missing, along with an antique table, of great sentimental value, that she got years ago in Spain . Three sets of king sheets and a brand-new duvet cover are missing as well …"

"We'd hardly need to take *her* sheets!" This round is lasting an awfully long time, but there's no hope of a referee, so I have to invent one.

"Well, I'm sure she'll be clear and fair about what needs fixing and repairing, and she'll send you a list, along with the bills, so you'll see what's what."

"*Nothing* is what's what!" she shrieks.

She's the heavyweight. She's a shrink. She is rich and lives on Park Avenue and has a second home in Venice, where she gives lectures in abnormal psychology. I am a lightweight by any standards, especially these.

"We cleaned the rugs and sofa," she continues. "We left that place in better condition than we found it." Now she's mad. She means to get me on the ropes.

All summer long, this woman complained. She called to complain about the air-conditioning and about the pile of garbage that hadn't been picked up (since she'd failed to set up service). She complained about the air-conditioner not being cold enough or the pool heater not being hot enough. She complained about the quality of dishes and silverware. And when, at the very last minute, when the leases needed to be signed and I had done everything within my power to satisfy both parties' demands, her husband threatened me: "If you don't get the leases out *immediately, this minute*, we will sue you! And your company!" I thanked him for his patience and said I was sure they'd have a good summer in the home. He hung up on me.

The woman complained all through July and into August. She had a staff of five people whom she instructed to complain as well. Housekeepers and chauffeurs called me to leave threatening messages. She called from Venice to warn me that the air-conditioning had better be really frigid by the time she returned. Her husband called warning me they'd sue if the pool wasn't heated to a constant temperature of eighty-one degrees. Her chauffeur called to say I'd better be at the house to open it up for the woman's sister, who was arriving that night at midnight. The housekeeper called to say she couldn't work the central vac. She was nearly in tears because the house had to be spotless for the woman's return.

The landlord called me to tell me I had better warn the tenant to stop calling her at home. The landlord's husband called to tell me his wife was having a nervous breakdown because of the awful people I'd put in their house. Their daughter called to tell me she'd driven by the house and seen garbage all over the yard that should be picked up. A day later, when it hadn't been, she called to tell me she'd done it herself and wanted money from the tenant to reimburse her for her trouble.

"So who asked her? It was our garbage. She had no business touching it! I'm not giving her a penny."

"Well, there are a few other issues," I say, returning to the business at hand.

"We left that awful house in better shape than it's ever been in … *what* other issues?! I can tell you right now I don't expect to see *any* bills!" (Meaning: No one dare call *me* on the carpet; the landlord was lucky to have me as a tenant.)

"Well, you see," I say, "it's mostly a problem of the carpets. There were exactly and precisely five piles of dog shit. *Dog shit*," I repeat, loud enough for her to get my drift. "Dog shit in the house. Since the landlord has no dog and it was not there when you took occupancy, it constitutes an issue—more precisely, five issues. So you see," I say, "I don't think the house was actually, literally, truly in better condition than when you took it. I mean, dog shit was not part of the furnishings; it wasn't exactly included in the rental, if you see what I mean. You can see what the landlord might be referring to when she says some cleaning and repairs might be in order, especially *if* you can understand that you swore on your mother's grave that those three teeny, tiny, itsy dogs were well behaved and would never cause any kind of damage … and that it might have been a good idea if you'd cleaned up the *dog shit* before you left. *If* you see what I mean …"

The bell rang, and she was down for the count.

I just heard a colleague on the phone with a customer, obviously trying to overcome objections to a house:

"You could throw in a pool, toss in some skylights, bang down that wall between the living room and the kitchen, and tear out the carpet. Privacy? That's easy—arborvitae it! No, I can't get you in there to look again right now. We must have an appointment; it's tenanted."

Violence! First to the house, and then to the English language.

MOST UNLIKELY

Elaine wears a red-and-white-striped strapless dress with a wide skirt, and Robert is dressed in a sleeveless undershirt with dark suit pants. She's carrying a small white dog and a large straw tote.

It's my turn—my "up," in real-estate parlance. "We're looking for an oceanfront house," Elaine says as they sit down at my desk.

"To buy, or to rent?" I ask, my blood pressure rising.

"To buy, darling, to buy." So I have hit the jackpot, and only eight months in the business.

Elaine and Robert are open to looking anywhere from Amagansett to Southampton, so they wait patiently while I put together the list of houses.

"I'll drive, if it's okay with you," Robert says.

"You sit in front," Elaine says to me as she gets into the backseat.

I give Robert directions to the first house, and as we're driving, I hear the sound of splashing water coming from the back of the car. I turn around to see what it is, and Elaine explains, "Oh, that's Lily drinking from her water fountain."

And sure enough, this small dog was happily lapping up water that was spilling from a fountain in the shape of a fire hydrant into a trough.

"Wow!" I say. "I've never seen anything like it!"

"Hammica Schlemma!" she shouts.

They hate the first house. "It needs too much renovation," Elaine explains. "I like modern, but this won't do. Let's get going."

On the way to the next house, I learn that Robert A. M. Stern designed their house in New York. "It's been in all the magazines," Elaine tells me. "I'll show you the next time, so you'll see what we like." I am dumbfounded. Looking at these people, she with her over bleached blonde hair in a messy bun and the zipper tearing away from the fabric in the back of her sundress, and he in his undershirt, I would never have imagined that these people could have appreciated Mr. Stern's sophisticated work.

They hate the next house and the one after that; in fact, they hate every house I show them over the course of a year. But during that time, whenever I'm with them, I learn something else about them, and I also learn that they are extremely nice people.

I learn that they have two dogs, three cats, five canaries, and a parrot.

"A parrot!" I say. "I love parrots! They're so funny and wonderful."

"Mean bird," Elaine says. "Mean bird, bite your finger off."

"Really?"

"Yeah. I used to hire someone to feed him and clean the cage when we traveled, but it got so I couldn't find anyone to do it anymore. When they'd go to put food in the cage, the parrot would peck down on them so hard, they'd be afraid to try again. Mean bird, bite your finger off."

"Oh, that's terrible."

"Yeah. So we have to take him with us."

"You travel with the parrot?"

"Yeah. What can I do? That bird's been to France, Italy, Israel, Spain ... and it seemed we always land at JFK on a Sunday!" Her voice gets shriller and shriller as she speaks, and the tempo quickens. "Do you have any idea how hard it is to find a vet to come to the airport on a Sunday? The bird has to be checked out before we can bring him back in the country! Impossible."

On another outing, I learn that they have a house in Atlantic Beach. They don't like it there any longer, and aren't using it.

"When we find a house out here, though, we'll still keep Atlantic Beach."

"I thought you didn't go there."

"We don't, but you see, we have three cats. They were all wild. We had them fixed. Two of them are fine, but the third one? It didn't take. So we're keeping the house in Atlantic Beach for him. We've hired someone to stay with him in the house until he dies someday. Then we'll sell. We can't put him down; he's an animal. And I can't bring him to the house in New York—he'd spray a Picasso!"

A year to the day from our first meeting, I call them and tell them about a new listing in Bridgehampton on the ocean, but tell them that it's rented, and we can't get in until after Labor Day. They don't care, they say; they'll come out to see it anyway from the outside.

We walk along the beach past the house. Back and forth we walk in the hot sand, she dressed in the same red-and-white striped dress, carrying Lily, and Robert still with the undershirt, but this time in khaki pants. We look, and I describe the layout of the interior, since the brokers in our office had been allowed in to see it the day before.

We walk around to the road in front of the house to see it from that angle, and then she says, "No. Not for us. Right, Robert?"

"You're right, Elaine. Not for us."

We drive back to my office, and before I leave them, I say, "I wish you would look at the house I showed you the first time out. It's still on the market. You really should look at it again."

"That place? No, it needs too much work."

"Please? Just look." They grudgingly agree to look again. I call the owner, who says we can come right over.

The house is an upside-down house, meaning that the living room, kitchen, dining room, master bedroom, and bath are on the top floor, along with a large deck and a spectacular ocean view, and the guest bedrooms and baths are on the first floor, with another large deck and fabulous view. The house is about eight years old and does need some updating, but it's closer to the ocean than the houses built later, after the setbacks changed.

We climb the stairs to the front door. Lionel opens the door, and I make the introductions.

When they go out onto the deck, Lionel whispers to me, "Can they afford this house?"

"Yes, Lionel, I'm sure they can."

"What does he do for a living?" he whispers.

"I don't know," I whisper back. "I've been trying to find out for a year, but the subject never comes up in conversation."

They go through the house carefully, upstairs and down. They thank Lionel, and we leave. When we're out in the driveway, Robert turns to me and says, "I'd like to make him an offer."

I almost keel over right there in the driveway, right there on the pebbles.

"Okay," I say, "let's go back to my office, and I'll call him."

"Can't we do it right now, as long as we're here?"

"Oh, okay. What would you like to offer?"

His offer is not far off the asking price. . "I'll raise my offer if need be, just so you know."

I run up those stairs two at a time. I give Lionel the offer.

He's dumbfounded. "Really?" he asks. "That's not what I want, but it's a good offer. Will they come up?"

"I believe they will." He makes a counteroffer. Down the stairs I fly with the counteroffer. Robert raises his offer. Up the stairs I go again, my heart pounding.

"Tell them they just bought a house," says Lionel. I run down again, this time tripping all over myself, and give them the news.

"Can we go up now and see what we bought?" Robert asks.

"Congratulations!" Lionel shouts. "This calls for champagne!"

"Oh, no," Elaine says. "It's only eleven thirty in the morning!"

"Come on," Lionel insists. "We have to celebrate." We all raise our glasses and toast each other, and then Lionel turns to Robert and asks, "So, Robert, what kind of business are you in?"

"Raincoats."

A broker on the phone talking about one of his exclusives to another broker who wants to show it: "I don't know, it's not an easy house to show. Every time I go there, even though I've made an appointment, the owner's mother is asleep on the couch in the living room, snoring loudly, and there's a bottle of gin on the floor next to her."

THE ONE THAT SLIPPED
THROUGH THE CRACKS

I show houses to Tom on and off for a little over a year. Sometimes he comes alone, sometimes with his young daughter. He calls if he's running late—something you'd ordinarily expect, but memorable because good manners seem to be a rarity these days. He never finds a house he likes, but he does find a woman he likes, so the next time I see him, he comes with his new wife, Polly. She's equally nice, making the time we spend together very pleasant, although the right house still eludes us.

A new listing comes on the market: a charming cottage located where they want to be, and listed in their price range. But do I show it to them? I do not. It's the house on Windy Lane, in which the owner killed his wife, cut her up, put her remains in a garbage bag, and drove her upstate, leaving the bag in a ditch somewhere. It was the horrifying town scandal about six years earlier. After the husband was caught and put in jail, the owner of my agency asked a few of us to come with him to the house to make an official appraisal for the estate.

A tangle of yellow tape surrounded the property, and the police accompanied us inside the house. Pieces of floor were cut out, leaving neat rectangles of missing wood in the living room and dining room. When we got to the mudroom, we found bloodstains on the floor. Overcome with nausea, I ran out of the house and onto the driveway before I got sick. I knew that if that house ever came on the market, no matter how they fixed it up, I'd never, ever show it; I'd never be able to go into it again.

Well, six years later, it's back on the market by the second set of owners. The first people who bought it after the murder renovated it, decorated it, and sold it. The present owners did a more extensive renovation, and I'm told that it's absolutely perfect. But those memories are too strong; I still want no part of it.

I call Tom and Polly a few months later when we get a new listing on a house that I know they'd like.

"Oh," says Polly, "we bought a house. I'm so sorry it wasn't from you—you worked so hard—but you didn't show it to us; I guess it must have just slipped through the cracks."

I'm crestfallen. "What house did you buy?" I ask, trying to keep the strain out of my voice. "An adorable house on Windy Lane," she answers, "exactly what we've been looking for."

For one second, I feel like telling her what happened in that house. I feel like telling her that the murderer died in jail and was buried in the graveyard right next to the house, but I don't. I wish them well.

Three months later, the house is on the market again. I make myself go in and look at it this time. It is, in fact, absolutely charming. I look at the floors. New. I wait for some reaction to set in. Nothing. It has been added onto in so many places, it isn't recognizable. The mudroom is even in a different location.

"Why are the owners selling?" I ask the broker.

"They don't spend enough time here," she says. "They go to Connecticut."

Later, I attend a party. I overhear some people talking about a house for sale on Windy Lane. I go over and listen. A woman is saying, "I asked the owners, you know what happened in your house, don't you? They didn't know, so I told them, and the next day, they put it on the market."

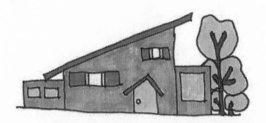

"Someone just gave me the finger," a colleague says, getting out of her car. "This must mean the season has officially started."

MOTHER HOOD

"What is that?" I ask. I am standing with prospective tenants on the second-floor balcony of a very important rental, looking down into the foyer.

"What?"

"Down there, by the door ..." I say, pointing. From far up, it looks like a bassinet, but I can't be sure.

"Oh, that's Tony Jr.," the woman with the long, black nails says. "It's okay."

"To *leave* him there?" The marble entry is ice cold and seems an unhappy place to leave a baby. The house, especially the foyer, is huge and, in February, freezing. "Don't you want to put him on the sofa, where it's warm?"

The two women look at one another. "I'm telling you it's okay ... okay? So just show us around ... *okay?*"

Before I can answer, they run on ahead of me. Suddenly, they reach out toward a light panel.

"Oh! Don't touch that!" I yell. "It's very complicated. If you touch the wrong button, the alarm will go off—"

Too late. I hold my breath and put my hands over my ears. Nothing happens.

"No big deal," one of them says. Unlike the other woman, heavily made up and very well-defined, this one looks like a line drawing. She has long and thin black hair and extremely white skin and is wearing a retro-looking velvet coat that drags on the floor. "We have this same system ... no big deal. I know how it works."

Whew! I can rest easy.

They resume running ahead of me, but because of the hardware on their boots and bags, I can more or less approximate their location in the house.

They continue to fly on ahead, turning on all the lights. They turn on the lights in the closets; the hallways; all the bedrooms and baths; the library; and the office; and, when we finally arrive back downstairs, they turn on the lights to the butler's pantry, the half baths, the kitchen, the den, and even the sunroom, which is flooded with natural light.

By this time, the one with the long, black nails is lagging behind, examining her reflection whenever she meets a mirror and snapping her cell phone open and closed, clearly annoyed that she's received no calls.

Once we're together in the living room (with the baby just around the corner, clearly forgotten), the woman with the nails asks if the owner is negotiable.

"The house is $700,000 for the season. What did you have in mind?"

"Well, like something off ... like *something* ... to sweeten the deal," she says, examining her nails. The other woman—who I have learned in the process of running through the house, is her sister—is standing behind her with a strange smile on her bloodless face. *What difference, I wonder, can "anything off" possibly make to people looking in this price range?*

I am losing my patience. I'm facing at least an hour's worth of work turning off all the lights and checking to see that nothing has been disturbed. Plus, I don't much countenance people who neglect their children.

"Seven hundred thousand dollars firm," I say. "Not a penny less."

They look at one another. "Well, maybe it'll do," the one with the nails says.

"For what?" I ask. Just then her phone rings. She snaps it open, relieved, and walks into the den for privacy.

"For her wedding," her apparition of a sister says. "Her and Tony. Like we have this big family, and this place would probably work."

"You mean you want to have a wedding *here*?" I ask. I imagine hundreds of women with long nails and lots of makeup running through the house, their heels tearing up the expensive carpets and their red wine staining all the white couches—not to mention the electric bill with this enormous family turning all the lights on and off at all hours of the day and night.

She gives me her enigmatic smile, but no answer.

Her sister returns. "Tony says we should just go ahead and take it. He'll pay the $700,000 if I want it ..."

"Do you?" I ask, staggered by this woman's power over Tony. But it doesn't really matter: I know the owner would never—no matter what they offer—rent to a family of gypsies (as I am now sure they are) who will wreak havoc with the electrical system and the Persian carpets.

As we're saying good-bye at the door, the mother remembers the baby and walks over to the bassinet. She pushes back the top and removes what I now see is a doll.

"She's due in June," her sister says. "She's practicing."

But why? I wonder. *The woman is a natural!*

Standing by their car, the sister puts the carrier and "baby" in the backseat, and the "mother" straps the baby in.

"We'll let you know," they say in unison as they drive off in their new-model Mercedes, which is black with tinted windows.

"The freezing compartment in this refrigerator is not working! The ice cream isn't hard enough! What am I supposed to do? You tell the landlord I won't stand for this!"

"I'll get someone over to fix it tomorrow. Today is Sunday, and I won't be able to reach the repairman. Meanwhile, though, right next to the laundry room is the door to the garage. There's an extra freezer in there."

"Are you kidding? You expect me to walk all the way to the garage?"

FANTASYLAND

He sits down in the chair beside my desk, clears his throat, and asks in a husky voice, "Do you have any big houses on the ocean?"

"Why, yes, I do," I reply, thinking how glad I am that I changed my dentist appointment. "Do you know the area, and do you have any preference as to which town?"

"It doesn't matter, as long as it's a big house and it's on the ocean."

"Fine," I say, "then I assume we're talking about at least six thousand square feet, right?"

"At least," he replies, shifting in the chair and adjusting the large brass belt buckle that seems to be boring into his paunch.

I put the information into the computer, making the starting price $15 million and the top price unlimited. Five houses come up in the search.

"Okay," I say, "here's one in Wainscott. It has six bedrooms and six and a half baths. It was built in 1987 but renovated in 2005. It's six thousand square feet, and it's on .90 acres. How does that sound?" I didn't tell him the price.

"Does it have a helicopter pad?"

"A *helicopter pad?* No, it doesn't."

"I need a helicopter pad."

Doesn't everybody? I think. "Oh, you didn't tell me that," I say. "That changes the picture."

"And I want it in the best part of the Hamptons—the very best, you understand?"

"Well, I'm sorry to say that none of these have helicopter pads. That's not a common thing here."

He seems a bit agitated. "Okay, if it doesn't have one, I'll build one. Let's see what else you got."

"I'll check into it for you, but I seriously doubt the town would let you build a helicopter pad. They have very strict rules. Why don't we see if you like any of the houses I have to show you?"

"You're trying to tell me there are no houses anywhere here on the ocean that have helicopter pads? I can't believe that!"

"Wait a minute!" I say excitedly. "I remember once showing an oceanfront house in Bridgehampton to a customer, and across the street from this house was the bay, and helicopters used to land right there in the bay. But that was years ago. I don't know if they still do that."

I am thinking of the time that a customer, a famous clothes designer, asked if I could find her a beautiful oceanfront house where they could do a fashion shoot. I called everyone on the ocean until I found someone willing to do it, and she was thrilled when she saw the place. She said she so appreciated the work I'd done to find this house and that she'd call her office and make arrangements to rent the place for the shoot. She then said that she would be staying in the year-round rental house I found her on the bay for a couple of more years, but then she'd be in a position to find something much more extravagant.

"Don't you worry," she said, "maybe it will be two more years, but then you'll sell me a place like this one, I promise."

Meanwhile, for the next two years, she wanted me to show her everything that came on the market that was on the water, either ocean or bay, and during that time, I got to know her fairly well.

One day, I had called her to tell her about a new listing when she said in a dismissive voice, "Never mind—I bought the house I'm in," and hung up. But I digress.

"Find out," he orders. "Find out if the helicopter service still exists. What else you got?"

I look for other houses on Dune Road, which seems like the only possibility. "Here's one," I say. "Ten thousand square feet, eight bedrooms, nine baths, pool, on an acre, $50 million dollars."

"$50 million!" he cries. "$50 million?" He waggles his forefinger, beckoning me to come closer as he leans in toward me, our heads almost touching. In a highly conspiratorial tone, he whispers, "I'm lookin' for someone with blood on their hands." With that, he sits up straight.

I remain frozen in my position, leaning over my desk, my head still down. "Oh!" I say cheerfully, recovering my composure as I sit back up. "Blood! Okay, blood you want, blood it will be! Uh, let's see ..." I turn to the computer, knowing full well that no matter how hard I might look, there's no "blood" category in there.

At that moment, a short woman with very long, very black, wavy hair in stiletto heels and a tight, white dress walks down the hall and stops at my desk.

"Honey," she says putting her hand on the back of his neck, "where ya been? I been lookin' all over for ya!"

"Gotta scram," he says as he stands up and takes her hand, and off they go.

"Isn't this a great laundry room?" I ask my customers as I look around the spacious, tiled, softly scented room with two industrial-sized washers and two dryers to match; the shelves of detergents, fabric softeners, dryer sheets, and bleaches; the cabinet for the fold-down ironing board and iron; and the flat-screen TV.

And as I'm standing there, in all this state-of-the-art glory, pointing out the myriad of virtues of the room, a pair of lacy underpants lands on my head from a laundry chute in the ceiling.

A DAY WITHOUT SUNSHINE

At one o'clock on a Wednesday in July, I open the door to one of my sales listings. I'm meeting another broker and her customers at one fifteen. I open the sliders, turn on the bathroom and bedroom lights, fluff the pillows, and throw the dead flowers in the garbage.

The sun shines on the turquoise pool. It shines on the water across the way. Sailboats glide in the harbor. The hydrangeas are in full bloom at the front of the house. I wait. At one thirty, I check my cell to see if the broker has called to say they're running late—nothing. Finally, at two o'clock, I close the sliders and turn off all the lights in the house, and just as I am starting to lock up, the broker drives up, jumps out of the car, and runs to me, all smiles and apologies.

"I am *so sorry*! *Sooooo sorry!* We got lost. And then we got lost even further," she says, laughing and turning to her customers, who now appear from the backseat, holding out their hands to be introduced. "This is Stephen," she says, "and Peckie."

I look carefully to see who is who. Stephen could be a girl, or a guy, or both. It isn't that he has on makeup or anything; it's just that he doesn't seem to represent a definite gender. The oddly named Peckie, on the other hand, is so thin she seems adolescent. She can't weigh more than fifty pounds. She has on a white sun visor and under it her hair is sticking up every which way, as if she almost electrocuted herself with the hair dryer.

They walk on ahead of me into the house. Peckie has on huge white sandals that look like cement blocks, so her "walking" is actually more like dragging. She is also having trouble talking due to what looks like a recent lip enlargement.

It takes a long time for them to go through the house (due, no doubt, to Peckie's shoes).

"Is she all right?" I ask the broker while Stephen and Peckie are dragging themselves around upstairs.

"What do you mean?" the broker asks. She is loaded with energy and is terribly enthusiastic about her new real-estate business, which she's been in now for a total of six months. "Oh, well, she is thin, but very determined ..." the broker adds, as if determination explains Peckie's weightlessness and her odd choice in shoes.

When the two return to the living room, Peckie opens all ten blinds in the front room. Turning to her husband, she faces him down with her hands on her hips.

"Well, sweetie," he says, "we *could* get shutters ... or awnings."

"Too much sun here," the broker says, crossing to Peckie and putting her arm around what should be Peckie's waist but what looks more like a thimble. Maybe Peckie's name is her nickname, short perhaps for Puckish ... or maybe Peckish. I can see the veins in Peckie's pale, white face, and I wonder if she has some rare disease.

"Well, we have to get to the next house," the broker says, pushing the two of them toward the front door. "It's on Elybrook," she adds. "Do you know where that is?" Obviously, six months in the business hasn't been enough time for her to find the northwest and its streets. I give her directions, but warn her and her customers that there is sun in that area also.

"Yes," the broker says, "but we've seen the photos on the Web and the house is very, *very* dark. It might be perfect!"

"Thank you," Peckie says, holding out her small, white hand, "but this is really *way* too light. Especially with the sun reflecting off the water."

"Oh, that!" I say. "Of course. You poor thing! Let's get you out of here right away."

"I'll deduct the utilities from the security deposit," the landlord says, "but I'm going to charge the tenants an administrative fee."

MY MAIDEN VOYAGE

It's late November 1980 and I've been in real estate for exactly two months when Valerie calls. She wants to buy a house, she says, and she would like to come out with a friend, a man she works with. They will be buying it together as an investment and renting it for some years, and then, hopefully, they'll sell it at a profit.

I prepare for this appointment; I prepare for two weeks. I look at every house in their price range, select the houses to show them, learn all the facts about each one, test the keys, learn the alarm codes, learn where not to let the cat out or the dog in, and then put the houses in geographical order. I do three practice runs. I have it nailed.

When we all get into the car on that long-awaited day, I completely forget where the houses are. I drive too slowly; in fact, I lose my grasp on how to drive and talk at the same time. I keep passing the streets where I should have turned. I make U-turns; I back up. In a sweat, I chat away while one part of my brain tries to remember where the hell we're supposed to be going next.

"Oh, this is beautiful!" the man says as we enter the last house on the list. "Does the carpet come with it?" I turn around to smile at him, thinking, *Here's a guy with a sense of humor.* The carpeting is wall-to-wall orange shag, dating from the fifties. Then I see his face: he means it! I tell him it does.

This is the one, they say; they love it. We go back to the office, and they give me their offer; I call the owner, and he makes a counteroffer; they accept, and I have a deal. A deal! I can't believe it—a novice with a deal! I recommend a few lawyers. They call one then and there, we all kiss good-bye, and they leave for New York.

It's mid-December, about a week before the closing, when I receive a call from my customers. They have been telling a friend about this investment house they're buying, and she wants to be in on the deal.

"Is it legal to have three people on the contract?" they ask me. I tell them it is. "Okay, then have her name added ... but she wants to see the house first."

The only day she can come out is Christmas Day, she says when she calls me. "I hope you don't mind," she says. My house will be filled with family and friends that day, but I tell her of course I don't mind.

The redheaded, mink-clad Rita sweeps into the living room that snowy Christmas morning, looking very much like a cocktail lounge chanteuse, which I believe she is.

She loves the house. I breathe again. The closing that has been delayed for her can finally take place.

Rita receives the contract the day before the closing and calls me. "I can't possibly buy that house," she says. "I wasn't aware that the house number is 135. That number is very bad for me. Unless the number is changed to 137, I can't invest. See what you can do."

Well, this never came up in real-estate school.

The following day, I speak to the postmaster and explain the situation. He seems to take it in stride and asks me to check back with him in an hour.

"You know," he says when I return, "it's the strangest thing, but this house was supposed to be number 137 all along."

"What do you mean there are no more village beach stickers?"

"They're sold out. It happens every year. That's why I told you to get one early and why I sent you the forms and the e-mail reminding you."

"I don't *care* if they're sold out! *You* rented me a house, now *you* get me that sticker! I'll pay whatever it takes! If I don't get a sticker, I'll badmouth your name all over town!"

A SEMBLANCE OF RESEMBLANCE

"The Stetzels told us to call you," an excited person said. "We're looking to buy, but we're not sure we can get something nice in the Hamptons in our price range ..."

Uh-oh, I thought. *Here it comes.*

"We can spend up to $3 million," she said, assuring me that something small would do. It was just for the two of them. Biking distance to the ocean would be nice.

"A pool?" I asked. I had come to think of this question as rhetorical.

"No," she said. "A pool isn't necessary."

"Would you be free on Saturday?" she asked.

"Absolutely!" I told her. I had a plethora of nice, small houses priced at up to $3 million with no pool and within biking distance of the ocean.

"How do we find you?"

"We're right on Main Street," I said.

"I mean your village—how do we find it?"

"Where are you from?" I asked, thinking it must be the moon.

"New Jersey," she said.

She called me another seven times between her first call and our appointment. She called to tell me they had no pets. She called to tell me her husband wanted little or no yard. She called to tell me they'd heard about an area called the Dunes, and they'd like to look there. Finally she called to tell me her friends had once rented in Montauk, and they said it was pretty down-to-earth. Could they look there, too, since she considered herself and her husband to be down-to-earth people?

So now we were set to look from Southampton to Montauk for a three-bedroom house with no yard, no pool, close to the ocean, with down-to-earth neighbors.

They got on the road on Saturday at seven. She called at ten to tell me they'd found a shortcut. She called at eleven to say they were in Riverhead, and was that close? At noon she called to say they'd arrived but were hungry; would it be all right if they got something to eat first?

By one thirty, I had called three times to rearrange appointments with owners.

"Who *are* these people?" one person asked on my third call.

"They're from New Jersey," I said.

"Oh," he said and hung up.

At one forty-five, they called as they drove by the office, looking for a place to park. At two, they materialized. We were only three hours late for our first appointment.

I met the husband, who looked a bit like Terence Stamp, and his wife, who seemed to be on speed, and we set out. But first they had to use the bathroom—and *then* we set out. She apologized for being late.

It was January, so unless I zoomed around the ten houses I had to show them, it would be dark by five. So I rearranged the schedule yet again, made a few calls, and narrowed the list to only the best of the houses.

"That damned shortcut," they both said in unison. They were talking over and to one another so that they missed Amagansett when we drove through.

"Are we still in Wainscott?" the husband wanted to know, looking, in profile, more than ever like the movie star. He had on those silver one-way sunglasses, meaning he could see out, but I couldn't see in.

"No, just going through Amagansett," I said, pointing out the farmer's market and the lanes. "That big block of blue you see there down at the end of the street," I said, emphasizing its accessibility, "is the *ocean!*"

"We have one in New Jersey ... same one," he said and turned to the backseat to talk to his wife.

"Too tacky," he said about the first house. "Badly built. Let's go," he said to his wife, taking her upper arm in a death grip and dragging her out of the kitchen while she was in the middle of telling me about the dreadful houses they'd seen in other areas of Long Island.

"... and for more money!" she yelled back over her shoulder as he pushed her into the backseat of my car. I was at the front door, apologizing to the owner for our abruptness in leaving.

We headed to the Dunes, down the slippery slope of icy, unplowed roads.

"You don't have four-wheel drive?" he asked in astonishment, taking his metallic sunglasses off for the first and only time and looking at me as if I were in boot camp and he was my squadron leader.

"Not to worry," I said, my wheels spinning, their rubber burning. Back in the backseat, his wife was saying how much the Dunes reminded her of New Jersey, and that was just what they *didn't* want:: too cramped, houses too close together.

"Let's get out of here," the husband said, insinuating that by not moving, I was deliberating keeping them in the area.

I took my foot off the accelerator and spent a quiet moment in meditation. "Ummmmmmmmmmm," I said. The car rolled off the icy patch, and suddenly we were free. "I think you'll like this next house," I said, skipping the others and going right to the best house of the lot. They'd fall in love; we'd have to go no farther. "It's everything you said you want: three bedrooms, a very small yard, a bike ride to the ocean, and no pool ... on one of the very best streets ... and well within your budget!" In fact, the house was a jewel and had been featured recently in *Architectural Digest*.

"We saw something like this in New Jersey" the husband said, walking disdainfully around the kitchen and running his hand slowly over the granite countertops, the kitchen lights bouncing off his sunglasses, "only it was more money ... probably better built." He opened the custom-made cabinets and drawers. "What kind of wood is this, anyway?"

"Rosewood," I said. "The very best wood there is ..."

The owner appeared and explained that the cabinetmaker was from the city and had been hard to get, since he worked on so many high-end kitchens.

"The yard's awfully small," the Terence Stamp look-alike said, looking out the windows at the frozen white tundra. I reminded him they'd asked for a small yard.

"No maintenance," I said.

"I like gardening," he said. I looked at his wife, who had clearly neglected to tell me about his hobbies.

"Come look!" his wife yelled a minute later from the back bedroom. "Isn't this the *exact* same bed the Glovers have?"

"Theirs is bigger," her husband said, "but yes, it's identical."

"Probably not," the owner said, appearing in the doorway. "We had it copied from a bed we saw in Italy. I think it's one of a kind."

The husband laughed. "Whatever."

Back in the car, with the best house behind us, I told him he looked like a famous actor.

"Terence Stamp," I said.

"Who's he? Never heard of him."

"He's very famous. Everyone knows him, probably because of his role as the main character in *Priscilla, Queen of the Desert.*"

"I never heard of it."

"I can't *believe* you don't know that movie." I looked at him in shock. "It's about a group of drag queens. Stamp played the main character. He wore the most fantastic costumes and this wild makeup. He made a fabulous-looking woman. You really should see the movie. It's incredible how much you look like him."

His wife leaned forward from the backseat to whisper to me. "David ... David," she said ever so softly, "is a little intolerant."

"No, I mean it," I said. "The resemblance is amazing. You should see the film."

It had grown dark, and Montauk was now out of the question.

I'm sitting here looking at a photograph a landlord found in his garbage and brought in to me. It shows the family I rented his house to posing in front of the pool with their Labrador retriever. They are all smiling—including the dog. The phone rings.

"You've got to do something. The landlord kept our entire security deposit; he said we had a dog, and that the dog dug up his yard. We don't have a dog—he's crazy! Please talk to him and get our deposit back!"

OPEN HOUSE

I arrive early, tying the brightly colored helium balloons at the end of the driveway on my Open House sign. I turn up the thermostat to a comfortable seventy degrees, arrange the bundles of flowers I bought into their vases, and place the vases in appropriate spots around the house.

"Am I too early?" a man's voice calls out.

"No, no!" I say. "Come in; you're right on time."

"Marty Bowen," he says, offering his hand. He's a short, solidly built man in his mid-fifties—the type you'd see on the tennis court or running on the side of the road in shorts in the winter.

"Have a look around," I say, handing him the color brochure of the house, "and if you have any questions, please ask."

Just then, the door opens, and two more people come in. "We're neighbors," they declare. "We're not interested in buying, but we always wanted to see inside this house. How much are they asking?"

I tell them, offering them a brochure. "Will you sign in, please?" I ask all three, motioning to the sign-in sheet on the table. As they sign in and walk into the dining room, two women arrive.

"Hi, we were passing by and saw your sign. We're not in the market, but we love to look at houses—hope it's okay."

"Of course it's perfectly okay," I answer. "Have a look around, and please sign in for me." *The lookers-as-sport and the neighbors: the two main categories of open-house attendees,* I think, *but that's fine—you never know.* I remember selling a house years before to someone who just came to an open house because she liked looking. She wasn't in the market, but she fell in love.

"You mustn't miss the garden when you're finished looking inside," I say, handing the woman a brochure. "Here's a picture of how it looks in the summer—it's absolutely glorious."

People come and go, keeping me very busy. When it quiets down, I go into the kitchen to find Martin Bowen sitting on one of the high stools at the marble counter, eating a sandwich. It was on one of the owner's plates, and he had a glass of soda in front of him, with the empty bottle sitting on the counter to his right.

I stop in my tracks. "What are you *doing?*" I ask incredulously.

"I'm having my lunch," he answers nonchalantly, wiping his mouth on one of the owner's cloth napkins. Seeing the expression on my face, he explains, "When I see a house I like, I try to get the idea of how I'd feel if it were my house. Would I be comfortable having a sandwich here? Reading a book here? You get the idea."

Good thing I found him before he decided to check out the water pressure in the shower.

From landlord to his winter tenant:

"Because of you not letting the broker show our house for August, I lost a $75,000 rental, so you and your cougar girlfriend are now at risk of a $75,000 lawsuit. You and your cougar girlfriend should read the f'n lease! If the house is a complete disaster and not well kept because of your nasty dog, I am telling you for the *very last* time, you're going to be sued! I don't know what that pathetic girl is paying you to f-ck her. The lease does not require twenty-four-hour notice to show the house, which you'll see if you read the f'n lease. We will have you forcibly removed. I will call the police, you lazy f-ck. No more Mr. Nice Guy from me. I am sick of your irresponsibility, and God knows what you and your nasty dog have done to our house, which you and your cougar girlfriend will pay for. Don't screw with me, or you and your cougar girlfriend will severely regret it personally, financially, and professionally. Get it, you irresponsible f-ck? Get out of our house!"

SELLER'S REMORSE

"We'll be friends," Paulo says, "I know it. You'll come over for dinner when I buy a house. I'm a good cook; we'll have fun."

I've been renting houses to Paulo and his partner, Frank, for two years, and now they are determined to buy a house and move out of New York City; they need a change of lifestyle, they say. They're looking for a small house with charm.

"It can need work—that's okay," Paulo says. "Frank can do anything."

It's the perfect place, a small cottage dating back to the early 1800s. I learn that it was moved from Montauk many years ago to its present location, and that it used to be an immunization clinic.

They love it. It needs work, they agree, but they absolutely love it, and they buy it. Paulo gives the orders; Frank does the renovation. And we have dinners together, as promised, in their house and in mine.

Years go by, and their lives change. They decide they want to fulfill a fantasy of theirs and run a bed and breakfast, so they need a larger house. They give me the exclusive on their house and tell me the price they want, saying, "We're not at all negotiable; this price is firm!" It is a fair price; they aren't gouging, yet they're making a nice profit.

I list the house and call customers of mine who have been looking for many months for a small, charming house.

"You know we're not going to negotiate," Paulo says when I ask if one o'clock the following day would be okay.

"I know," I assure him.

"Who are these people? Do they know the house is small?" I explain that I've been working with them for quite some time, that I know what they're looking for, that I told them all about the house, and that they want to see it.

Paulo greets us at the door wearing a large, bulky sweater with a down jacket over it. It's autumn, and it's cold … but not that cold. We walk through the kitchen door; the husband goes in one direction and the wife in another. Since it's such a small house, it takes no time to see it all.

As the wife walks down from the upstairs bedroom, she looks at her husband for a second, and he turns to Paulo and says, "We'd like to buy your house."

"I'm not negotiable," he answers.

"I understand. We'd like to buy your house."

"Do you feel how ice cold it is in here?" Paulo asks. "I feel as if I'm getting pneumonia—I can never get this house warm enough."

"That's okay—we'd like to buy your house."

"Sit down," Paulo orders. "Now, just put your hand on the wall behind you. Do you feel how cold it is? I don't think there's any insulation in this place."

"That's okay."

"No, feel it! Touch the wall!" The husband touches the wall dutifully. "I'm shivering all the time. It has this wood-burning stove that just gives a little heat, but it's not nearly enough. And," he says, turning to me, "did you tell them that we had that termite infestation recently?"

"That's okay," the husband repeats calmly. "We'd like to buy your house."

"When they moved it here originally, this was a small dirt road, and now - listen, do you hear the traffic? It whizzes by all the time, day and night."

"That's all right."

"You know the cellar has a dirt floor, and it's very small. I'm sure animals live in there; it gives me the creeps. Don't you want to go down there?"

"No," the husband says. "I don't have to."

Paulo eventually gives up and stutters, "Okay, okay! It's ... it's a deal."

They shake hands, and we leave. Talk about seller's remorse!

We go around the room at the weekly office meetings and let the others know about any new information we have: a new listing, a drop in price, and so on.

Harry has an exclusive on the Bennett house, which has been languishing on the market for more than two years. When his turn comes, he announces happily that Bennett has finally accepted an offer. Everyone applauds, happy for Harry—and happy that we don't have to hear about the Bennett house any longer.

The following week, Harry makes two announcements in the order he deems most important: "The Bennett deal is dead. So is Bennett."

PEETA AND SHELLY

"Is this the masta?"

"Yes, this is the master bedroom," I answer.

"Oh, Peeta! Get me outta heah—I can't stay heah another minute!"

I'm showing rentals to Shelley and Peter. They've never been to East Hampton. They just heard the words "the Hamptons" and knew that if they are to keep their social status, whatever that is, they better rent a summer house immediately.

We go to the next place. Although I'm showing them houses in the price range they requested, one look at Shelley tells me that she has better things in mind. She came dressed for the occasion, done up in faded denim, leather with fringes, cowboy boots, lots of silver and turquoise, and long, pearlized nails protruding from limp hands held shoulder-high, dangling from arms bent at the elbow. Get the picture? Peter keeps a lower profile. He's also dressed in jeans, but has on a simple white shirt opened just enough to show a touch of chest hair and two gold chains around his deeply tanned neck.

They look at four or five more houses. Shelley rejects them all. "Peeta! Look at this house, it's so small! I could nevva stay in such a place!"

"Shelley, it's a beach house for a month. It's nice, it's clean, and we're not buying it—it's a nice beach house." She flashes him a look. "Okay," he says, "show us what we could get if we spend more money. A house with a pool?"

"You know," Shelley says to her husband as we are driving, "if we take a more expensive place, we could share it with Carol and Jerry."

"Good idea," he agrees.

As we enter the next house, and she sees the difference in size and decor, Shelley exclaims, "This is at least nice! Where's the masta?" She buzzes through the house in no time, the heels of her boots clicking on the Italian tile floors. She opens closets and cabinets, bounces on the couches, lies down on the beds, checks for cross-ventilation, and finally, finding things to her taste inside, goes out on the back deck to check out the pool area. "This happens to be nice," she pronounces.

"You could enta-tain. Do they enta-tain in the Hamptons?" I tell her that there's a lot of that going on.

"That does it!" Peter declares. "You get what you pay for. Show us the next-level house. I want a better house."

"But Peeta," Shelley protests, "this one is okay. We can share it with Carol and Jerry and enta-tain!"

"No, I want to see a better house."

So off we go again, this time to one of the most expensive houses that rents in that area. It's an all-white, contemporary, three-level affair with a spectacular ocean view from the two top floors. The ground-level floor has a living room, bar, bedroom, bath, and sliding doors to the deck and pool.

"This happens to be very nice," whispers Shelley, awestruck.

"Wait—you haven't seen anything yet. Follow me," I say, getting into the whole thing after spending three hours in their company. I lead them up to the next floor, the location of four of the bedrooms, my hands dangling limply from arms bent at the elbows.

Shelley enters the largest bedroom and declares it "gawjus." "This is the masta!" she exclaims.

"No," I correct her, "this is Carol and Jerry's room!"

"I don't believe it—this isn't the masta?"

"Come on, you'll see!" I'm beginning to enjoy this.

As we climb the stairs to the top level, Shelley's voice behind me is barely audible. "Now this" she says, "this is a tsotal en-*vi-ron*-ment!"

"Didn't I tell you? Now, come, take a look at the masta!" I command. They follow me across the living room, Shelley's and my hands flapping up and down with each hurried step.

"Peeta, this is as nice as our house at home!"

"Shelley, this is *nicer* than our house at home. We'll take it. We'll tell Carol and Jerry to come out tomorrow to look. They'll love it. Then you'll send us a lease."

Somewhere on the Long Island Expressway, reality must have struck. I never hear from them again. But that's okay. The phrase "tsotal en-*vi-ron*-ment" is mine forever.

"Wait until you hear this! I'm so excited! After four years, two months, and six days of looking—I just checked my diary to see how long we've been working together—I found the perfect house for you ... the one we've been searching for all this time!"

"Oh, we bought a house. But you've been so nice, so if we ever decide to rent it someday, we'll give you the listing."

SAND IN MY SHOES

The call was from Nan and Dan, a couple from Philadelphia. Their niece had a house in the beach area of Amagansett known as the Dunes. They loved it there. They wanted a piece of land in the Dunes to build their own house.

Land. The word made me shudder. I had been in the business only four months, and although I knew what land looked like, I didn't have a clue how to sell it. There are no spacious living rooms with vaulted ceilings to rave about, no Italian marble, no state-of-the-art kitchens. What can you say about land? It's bright? It's airy? "Look at that sand! Did you ever? Feel how soft it is." Or in a wooded area, I supposed you could say, "Look at all those trees! Think of the shade—better for the skin than sun, you know." I was at a loss, but I was willing to take on the challenge.

They were coming in a week, so for the next six days, I learned land. I concentrated on the Dunes, but in case they changed their minds, I looked at land in several places.

All real-estate brokers have tax maps—large books with maps of every street, every block, and every lot. When listings are taken for a house, land, or a rental, besides the address and all pertinent information, the tax-map number is always included. After finding listings that met their criteria, I turned to the matching page of the tax-map book to find all these little squares indicating the different lots.

"Oh," I said, looking at the tax map, "this is easy. One of the pieces of land for sale is the one ... two ... three ... four ... *fifth* little square from the corner on the right." So I gathered all the land listings, and off I went with my trusty tax map by my side. When I got to my first lot, however, all I saw was sand. Lots and lots of sand. No neat little squares told me where one lot ended and the next one began.

"How the hell am I supposed to know where this one lot for sale is in the middle of this desert?" I asked aloud, speaking to no one. Since this was a new development, no houses had yet been built on the street. I did have the subdivision map with me, though, and walking from the beginning of the street, I paced off the approximate frontage of each lot to get an idea of where "my" lot was. This lot, if I could find it, seemed ideal for Nan and Dan. It was where they wanted to be, and they'd have an ocean view from the second story of their future house.

I then remembered the office had a measuring wheel. It was kept under the desk of the most intimidating broker—a mean-spirited, selfish woman who had been there for years and resented newer brokers. She hadn't said a word to me in the four months I'd been there, and she answered my "good morning" greetings with a glare. Knowing that she was out of town for a couple of days, I drove back to the office, snatched the measuring wheel, and raced back to the lot before the sun went down. From the map I was holding, I knew this lot started five hundred feet from the beginning of the road and ran along it for two hundred feet. I paced it off, picked up a shell, and put it at the beginning of the lot, and then paced off another two hundred feet and put a stone at the far end.

We drove straight to the Dunes the minute they arrived, and I stopped in front of the lot. I showed them where the lot began, at the shell, and where it ended, at the stone. We paced off the depth with the wheel. They loved it; it was exactly what they were looking for—better, in fact. The nature preserve area in front was more than they'd dreamed of. That, plus the potential ocean view made them more excited. They paced it off themselves. They walked to the far end of the lot, whispering together.

"We'll take it," they announced. "We love it. It's perfect."

I was elated; I was loving this business.

"We don't have to see any other lots," they told me. "This is the one. Now come and join us for lunch." I was selling a lot—my first one. Who could think of eating? They insisted. We ate, but I wasn't sure I'd be able to keep it down.

After lunch, we went back to the office, and I called the owner of the lot and left a message asking him to call me immediately. Nan and Dan asked me to call them as soon as I heard back, and they also asked me to send them a map of the subdivision.

The owner was thrilled with their full-price offer.

The following day, I sent out the memorandum of sale to all parties and their attorneys, along with the subdivision map Nan and Dan had requested. Three days later, I got a phone call.

"The tax-map number on your memorandum says it's lot number

nine, but the subdivision map says it's lot number eight. I don't understand. Could you clarify it for me?"

I was caught off guard. "Let me get the subdivision map and the tax map, and I'll call you right back." I compared the two maps. They were right: the numbers didn't coincide. The lot we'd paced off was lot number eight, right next to number nine. It was equally flat, equally shaped, and equally priced. In a panic, I asked my boss to take a look.

"Sometimes it happens like that," he said. "The numbers on the two maps don't match. You have to go by the tax map."

"Could you come with me to see these two lots?" I asked him. "I'm dying!"

"You just sold the wrong lot, my dear," he said with a laugh after we paced off the lots. "But," he added, "there is no difference between the two; they're absolutely the same. They can take my word for it."

"We couldn't buy a lot without seeing it," Nan and Dan said when I called.

"But you did see it," I tried to explain. "We walked right along the road, right past all the lots that are for sale. It looks exactly like the lot next to it—no difference whatsoever."

"We would have to see it," they repeated.

"Okay," I answered. "When can you come and look?"

"I don't know," Dan answered. "Wait a minute." I heard him ask, "When can we go out to Amagansett to look at the other lot?" When he addressed me again, he said, "Not for at least a month—we've got a very busy schedule." Of course they never came.

A group of us were taken on vacation for being the top brokers of the year.

Before going out and enjoying ourselves, we had to meet every morning at breakfast to discuss different aspects of the business. One morning, the topic was "Why do you think you've been successful?" We went around the table and each gave their idea. One of the brokers said she thought the reason for her success is that she treats all of her customers and clients as family.

When the meeting was over, and we were sitting around the pool out of earshot of our managers, a colleague of the broker said, "Tell them the real reason why you've been successful."

"I pee on the property."

"You *what?*" we shouted.

"Yeah, I pull down my pants and pee on the property. You know—I mark it. It works! Try it!"

THE WOMAN FROM MINNESOTA

"We don't do real estate that way here," I keep telling her every day when she calls: at my home at seven thirty in the mornings, and then again at noon, and finally and always, late at night, just as I am about to fall asleep.

"What about the security system? Is there well or town water? How much money do I bring to the closing? Where is the closing? Why isn't it where it's convenient for *me*?" Then, finally, after these annoying calls that go not just to me, but to her lawyer, to the seller's lawyer, and then, fatefully, to the seller himself, her questions turn even more frequent and frantic when she can't get the answers she wants. "*Why* won't he let us into the house? Why is his lawyer such an asshole? Why would he think I'd want to buy his awful old second-rate furniture anyway? How do I know he made the repairs he said he'd make? Can I get the engineer back for a second look? Will he pay for it? What do you mean they've changed the closing date?"

She keeps telling me, "We just don't do real estate that way where I come from," reminding me that she and her family have handled more real-estate deals than I could imagine, so she knows what she's talking about.

I feel like Alice falling down the rabbit hole. She hangs up on her lawyer. Then her lawyer hangs up on the seller's lawyer. Then the seller threatens to kill the deal and give her back her money. Then she writes him a threatening letter saying he was price gouging not only on his home, but the "tacky second-rate furniture" he'd offered to sell her at a discount. Her lawyer and his refuse to speak to one another; they also refuse even to fax or e-mail back and forth. I place a conference call at one point and have to scream at both lawyers to behave like adults.

"Let's keep our eye on the prize," I say to them at the point where the seller's lawyer is threatening to have her lawyer disbarred. "Eye on the prize," I keep saying, until at one point I lose all composure and scream at them to "Stop it!" as they continue to yell over one another.

My colleagues turn to stare. "Talking to children?" Susan asks when I hang up. She is the mother of three children, six, eight, and twelve, and knows the impulse to scream "Stop it," though I have never heard her do it.

The closing, of course, gets cancelled. The seller's lawyer says his client can easily sell the house to someone else—like a sane person. "For a lot more money," he adds.

I tell the buyer she has to stop harassing the seller if she wants the house. "Why has something so simple gotten so out of hand?" she asks, as if she is innocent of causing any problems. "Things are so simple in Minnesota," she says. "For instance, when my father, a *very* big commercial broker—"

But I cut her off. "Do you *want* this house?" I ask. "If so, I will try and resurrect the deal."

"Of course I want the house, but why is he being such an asshole?"

"*That's it!*" I say "That's the problem we're having. You've insulted him. No one here—unlike Minnesota—*has* to sell their house. If you continue to insult him, he will refuse to sell it to you."

"But the price he's asking for that stupid furniture—"

"That's not the point!" I scream.

Susan turns around to look at me. *Motherhood must be good preparation for doing real estate*, I think. *I've never heard Susan yell at a customer. I would be a terrible mother.*

I call both lawyers and get a conference call going. "I'll have you disbarred," the seller's lawyer yells at the other lawyer, and the other lawyer, a woman, starts to cry. "Women!" he says on the other end of the line.

"My customer wants to try and put this deal back together," I say. "She is sorry if she insulted anyone by making a fuss about the furniture."

"Fine. Fine," the seller's lawyer says. "But what about this insistence that he close the pool before she moves in? He's *still* using it. It's *his* pool." I have heard nothing about this; it was enough to hear about the furniture and to put out that fire.

The buyer's lawyer has now pulled herself together and stopped crying. "Well, he wouldn't sell his stereo system, so we don't see why she should have to pay for the pool being left open—"

"This is crazy," I say. "Forget the pool. Forget the furniture. Your client wants to sell his house. My customer wants to buy it. It's that simple. Let's set another closing date and get this done. Period. End of story." I hang up.

Susan, who by now knows this entire saga, asks if I think I did the right thing. At this point, I don't care. Susan is not sure about me. I can see her thinking I would make a really bad mother.

But a closing date finally gets set. We work out the problems with the furniture and the pool. Everyone meets at the closing and shakes hands. The buyer's lawyer turns out to be a very young woman who is too frightened to look anyone in the eye. The woman from Minnesota turns up in her best Minnesota duds, smiles, signs the checks, and doesn't say one inflammatory word. The seller, whose wife is divorcing him, makes us all wait an interminable time while he and his lawyer reconcile a missing eleven cents. His lawyer, when he stands to shake my hand, is revealed to be so short that I am sure he is standing in a hole.

For my part, I suddenly remember buying a house in North Carolina after moving there from New York. A very nice broker tried to explain to me how things worked differently and slowly in the south as I bombarded her with daily phone calls, insisting I knew real estate backward and forward, and that nothing she was doing was the way we did things in New York.

The key is under the Bilco door, the owner says, at the back of the house—the one that goes down to the cellar. I pull in the driveway, we get out of the car, and I ask my customers to wait at the front door while I get the key. I open the large metal door, and I'm greeted by earsplitting, bloodcurdling screeches. I jump back and look down, and there, on the top step of the cellar stairs is a bat, a small creature with large fangs, looking very much like a tiny devil, flapping its wings violently.

This job is not for the fainthearted.

THAT HOUSE IN AMAGANSETT

This very thin, thirtyish woman with lots of bangle bracelets tells me what kind of house she wants. She likes Amagansett and has to be south of the highway. She's willing to spend whatever it takes to get what she wants.

We drive around for about an hour, but I can only get us into two houses, since it's summer and most of them are rented.

"I just remembered a house I have to see!" she says. "I was shown it last year from the outside, but we couldn't get in, because there was a tenant in there. Is it still for sale?" She describes the house, and I know exactly the one she's talking about. I tell her it's still for sale, but it's rented for the season, so we need to make an appointment if we have any chance of getting in.

"Oh, *please!* Just pull in the driveway and let me see it—I want to make sure you know which house I'm talking about."

We pull in the driveway, and she shrieks with pleasure. "This is it! This is the house! If my husband won't buy it for me, I'll divorce him. I want this house."

With that, the front door opens, and out comes a man and his dog. "Can I help you?" he asks.

"I'm so sorry," I say, and I introduce myself and Madelyn, explaining that she just wanted to see the house on the outside for a second to make sure it was the one she had seen the year before, and that I hadn't meant to disturb him.

I've started to back up when Madelyn says, "Wait! Please let me ask you something. Is it a wonderful house? It looks wonderful. Is it as wonderful on the inside as it seems on the outside?" He answers that it's a very nice house and that he's happy he rented it.

Again, I have put the car into reverse when she stops me. "Wait! Let me ask you something," she calls out. "Are the rooms a nice size? Is it a sunny house?" He tells her it's spacious and sun-filled, and I apologize again.

As we're leaving, once again she calls out, "Wait! One last thing. Your dog. I want to get a dog for my daughter. What kind of dog is that? It's cute." He tells her the name of the breed and then she asks, "Is it intelligent?"

He looks down at the dog, pauses for a few seconds, and then looks up at her, and then back to the dog. "It's a dog." He shrugs. "I don't look to it for intellectual companionship."

As we're about to leave, he tells us that we can come in and see the house, but to please be quick and to start in the master bedroom, because he's working there and wants to get back to it.

There are piles of papers on the desk and a guitar propped up against the wall. *Isn't that nice,* I think to myself. *He's a writer, no doubt, and when he has to take a little break, he plays the guitar. Nice man.* When we finish looking at the master bedroom, he goes in and closes the door, and Madelyn and I inspect the rest of the house.

"This is a great house!" she declares. "I love everything about it! I want this house!"

There's a stack of mail on the kitchen table, and my curiosity takes over: I have to find out who this man is. Paul Simon. *Paul Simon!* And we're barging into his house? I can't believe it. I run outside and find Madelyn examining the pool.

I whisper, "Guess who that man is?"

"Who?" she whispers back.

"It's Paul Simon!"

"Who's Paul Simon?"

This is the last time I ever see Madelyn. Occasionally, I wonder if she and her husband are still together.

"The exclusive is almost over, and I'd like to send you an extension, if it's okay with you."

"No, I'm not going to extend it; I'm going to give it to someone else."

"But you didn't want to come down in price, even though the market has changed ... and now that you've reduced it and it's at the right asking price, you're taking it away? It doesn't seem fair."

"It's fair."

"But I've had so many open houses—I've spent a lot of time and money on it."

"I don't care, *you* didn't sell it."

SO MUCH MONEY, SO LITTLE TIME

The woman is looking for a July to Labor Day rental. "Money," she tells me over the phone, "is no object." She assures me that it must simply be a "nice" house, with eight bedrooms, close to the beach.

On Saturday she arrives with her driver, Gino, in a big black car with black windows. We meet at the first house, and she rolls her window down halfway. We talk while Gino keeps the motor running.

"I'll just run through this one," she says. She has a light, almost undetectable stammer, but when I see that she can't weigh more than ninety pounds, I figure there's a connection. She jumps from the car and literally runs through the house, talking all the while. I am miles behind her and can't possibly keep up. I have the sense something or someone is chasing her; something is scaring her to death.

"Too small!" she says of the first house and jumps back into the backseat of the car. Gino is ready to follow, so I fly from the driveway and almost kill us all by forcing my way into the bumper-to-bumper traffic on the highway. It's clear there's not a moment to lose. Not only is she frantic, but I am also frantic for her. She seems like a very nice woman at the mercy of someone or something, and I want to help her, to find her a house as quickly as possible, so she can get back to the city and rest.

When we get to the next house, she jumps from the car holding a magazine of rental properties to her almost concave chest.

"I can't leave a stone unturned," she confesses, and she asks me about three houses she's circled. The magazine looks as if it's been shredded, torn to bits by wild animals. I can just make out what and where the houses are and explain that one is already rented; the other two are in the woods.

"Nothing in the woods!" she shrieks, as if being in the woods would mean her sudden death. I look at my watch. We need to drive from here to there (a long way away in very bad traffic) and have only forty-five minutes left to do it.

"I'll just run through this one quickly," she says again, "though it looks small." I let her go alone; if I try and run with her, I'll only hold us up. Gino is standing beside the car.

"Did you have any trouble driving out?" I ask, making conversation while we're waiting. He smiles at me and winks. I imagine he doesn't speak English, though I don't know why he winked at me. Maybe it's a tic.

"Too cluttered," she says, throwing herself into the backseat of the car. So our two cars speed off. I keep her car in my rearview mirror and go as quickly as possible from the last "cluttered" house to one a town away. Clean and uncluttered, the house is less than fifty feet from the ocean. It's well furnished. It has eight bedrooms. There's a pool and a tennis court. Needless to say, it's a lot of money. Going through it, she slows down. Slightly. The sunroom, with its four down-filled white couches and its view over the dunes to the water, captures her in flight, and she says this might do. "But let's move on," she says, picking up speed and running back to the car.

Off we go again, this time back the way we came, nearly to Montauk, to what I hope is the pièce de résistance: a stark, white architectural wonder of a house, high on a hill above the ocean. It has ten bedrooms, eight baths, a vanishing pool, a tennis court, and a gourmet kitchen. There is even a guest cottage off on its own, down the hill and within spitting distance of the ocean. It's available for less money than the first house we saw, which was "too small."

"This could work, I think" she says, walking back toward the car, and I feel as if maybe, finally, we've accomplished our objective.

I get back in my car, ready to pull out and lead them back toward town and my office, when she suddenly re-emerges from hers. A minute ago, she looked as though she might be verging on serene; now—only minutes later—she looks more frantic than ever. Her hair is sticking up wildly. Her sweater is hanging off her in some sort of lopsided fashion, the buttons all in the wrong buttonholes.

"Mom ..." some voice from somewhere inside the car makes itself known. "*Mom!*" Gino, who is now standing beside the car, winks at me again as the voice and its owner spill out from the backseat of the car. This girl, who must be the woman's daughter, is four times her mother's size; she is unwrinkled and unperturbed, without a hair out of place. Her clothes look freshly washed and ironed. She towers over her mother.

"Why, hi," I say and introduce myself, but I am invisible. No one exists in the world right at this moment but this overweight girl and her mother.

Where has she been all this time? But then I know when I see a tiny silver phone—no bigger than a hearing aid—grafted onto her ear.

"Mom," she says, looking through me, oblivious to the day, the ocean, and anyone else's needs but her own, "Valerie is going to be staying in Southampton. We can't be here! *No one* will be here!"

Valerie is clearly on the other end of this tiny silver phone, telling this girl, her mother, the driver, and me what their *real* needs are for the summer.

"There is a house in Southampton …" I begin, "but it may be too small … and it's really awfully expensive for what it is."

"Let's see it!" the girl says to her mother. She walks past her mother and around to the driver's side of the car, the small phone still in her ear with Valerie on the other end, issuing orders and giving directions. It is understood—though no one says a word—that Gino is to give up his place so that she can drive.

"We'll follow you back," the mother says, and she and Gino get into the backseat together.

We head off, back the way we came, forty miles back to Southampton, to a $400,000 summer rental, back through the worst traffic we've had since the previous summer. What I don't realize until we're out of the drive and back on the highway is that this girl, who can't be more than fifteen, is not just driving; she's *learning* to drive. We're going about ten miles an hour, and if I am to keep them in sight and not lose them, it will take us about two hours to get where we're going.

I try to relax. I ignore all the honking behind our two cars, along with the dirty looks and gestures I get as cars try to get around us. If I don't relax and give up control, I could end up looking like the mother. I could end up with a stammer.

I try to look at the big picture: "money is no object," and Valerie is in control. They'll take the house in Southampton, because it suits Valerie and the daughter, and Gino will get a two-hour break before he has to get back in the driver's seat to return the mother and daughter to Manhattan.

Down the road and years from now, the mother's nerves will be totally shot, and she will be even smaller than she is now. The daughter will have slimmed down, but will still be angry. She will show up for Sunday dinners with her father and mother and accept, as if it's her due, the check they give her to keep her from hating them even more than she does now.

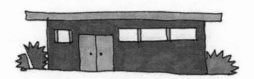

"You know the house the MacDonalds bought?"

"The one in Sagaponack?"

"Yeah ... they're renovating and adding a tennis court."

"But it *has* a tennis court!"

"Yeah ... but you can always use two. After all, there are two dishwashers, two Viking stoves, and two refrigerators ... so why not?"

Indeed. Why not?

THE CLOSING

The showings go well. They like four out of eight of the houses they see. Unlike so many customers, they tell me what they like about them and what they don't.

It always amazes me when customers won't talk to me, won't let me know if I'm on the right track or not when I select houses to show them. I decide that they must have made a pact before they meet me: "Whatever you do, don't let the broker know if you like a house." What could they be thinking? That the price will go up if I know they like a house? What would I do, call the owners and tell them that the customer likes the house and with that knowledge, the owners will stand firm at their price, even though they'd been prepared to negotiate? It's ridiculous, but it happens quite often.

Sometimes, as I'm driving along, I'll try to make conversation, and they'll answer monosyllabically.

"Hasn't the weather been terrific?"

"Yes." Pause.

"We're so lucky; other places have been getting a lot of snow."

"Yes." Pause.

"Have you been out here before? Are you familiar with the area?"

"Yes." Pause.

It goes on from there until I finally give up and we drive in silence to the next house.

"What did you think of the house?" Silence. "I thought it was nice and seemed to have everything you asked for ... did you like it?"

Pause. Finally, a very soft mumble: "It's okay."

Anyway, these customers make another appointment for next weekend to look again at the four they liked, wanting to put some time and distance between visits to enable them to absorb the details of each house.

The following Saturday, they come again.

"We think we've decided on the one we want," they say, "but we'd still like to see all four again, just to be sure."

"In any particular order?" I ask, pretty sure I know which house it will be.

"No, that's okay—take the route that's easiest for you."

What a pleasure, I think. *What a pleasure to get such a nice couple—so reasonable, and so friendly.* They look at all four and then tell me which one they want. It was the one I thought they'd choose.

"Can we go back and see it one more time?"

"Of course," I say, "take as much time as you like." It's a beach house with lots of windows, lots of light, a large wraparound deck, and a bit of an ocean view. After walking through it one more time, they come over and put their arms around me, thanking me and saying that I've made them both so happy. It's the best part of this business, matching the right house with the right people.

On the way back to the office, they tell me that they want to offer the full asking price. They say they think the price is fair, and they don't want to take the chance of losing the house to someone else. *It doesn't get any better than this*, I think, and it certainly makes up for the many, many customers who never buy after months, if not years, of looking. I call the owners and make the offer.

"We'll be using my brother as our lawyer," the wife says, "and we can close as soon as the seller would like."

"The sooner the better," the husband says. Everyone kisses and hugs, and they leave for New York.

"My brother wants to see the house," the wife says the following day. "Can we come out on Friday?"

"Of course!" I answer cheerfully, but cheer is not what I feel. I hear that voice in my ear, saying *Uh-oh!* It's been my experience that brothers, sisters, parents, friends, and whoever else the buyer brings to look at a house usually puts the kibosh on the deal.

"What are you thinking?" they say. "It's too much money!" Or, "You're paying *what*? For this? Look at the construction!" Then there's "The guest room is on the second floor. I'm too old to climb those stairs! Don't you want me to come and visit?" or "Did you ever think about what will happen when they build across the street one day?" and "My friend bought a house bigger than this for less money. You're being taken!" It goes on. I knew it had been too good to be true.

Ron, the brother, likes the house a lot—everything about it. In fact, he picks out the room he wants to stay in when he visits. I let out the long breath I hadn't even realized I'd been holding in.

They arrive for their walk-through the day of the closing. They

120

check the appliances, the heat, and the pool, go down to the basement, and declare everything is in order.

The papers are being shuffled around the table at the seller's attorney's office. Ron points to a clause in the contract and says, "We never agreed to this."

"But you did," the seller's attorney answers. "You and I had a conversation, and you agreed that the Coles could take out the chandelier over the dining-room table and replace it with a different one. Look, it's even in the memorandum of sale that we all got."

It certainly has been agreed upon, I think to myself. *What's he pulling?*

Ron raises his voice. "I'm telling you, we never agreed to this! My clients want the chandelier they originally saw over the dining-room table! That's not negotiable! Do you want to close this or not?" He glares at the other attorney and then at the sellers. "Well, do you?" he shouts.

The buyers sit there, expressionless, intently studying the grain in the wooden table.

"That chandelier was a wedding present to us from my parents," the seller says quietly. "I would never have agreed to leave it in the house. We put in a very lovely replacement. Didn't you see it when you walked through the house?"

"I didn't notice it," Ron says, turning to his sister. "Did you?"

"No," she answers, still looking down.

The seller's attorney slams his hand down on the table. "Well, unless you agree to taking the chandelier that's there, this meeting is over."

Ron stands up, looks at the attorney, and says, "Step outside," motioning toward the hallway. The attorney follows Ron out of the room, closing the door behind them. The next sound we hear is the crack of a slap followed by another, followed by the sound of a punch, an "ow," another punch, another "ow," and then a thud. Everyone looks at each other in jaw-dropping disbelief.

Moments later, the door opens, and both disheveled attorneys enter the room, blood trickling down the side of Ron's face from a cut near his eye.

"Sign the papers, damn it!" he shouts to his sister and brother-in-law. "You're getting the chandelier that's there!" And the closing is over.

"You see," a wealthy client says to his broker upon finally finding the house of his dreams, "I want the house, but I really have to sell my chateau first ..."

THE DAY, WEEK, MONTH,
YEAR MY SHIP CAME IN

I haven't been so lucky in a long time. I'm renting a house with three friends on Deer Isle, off the coast of Maine, where I've never been. I am far, far away from the nonsense of real estate in the Hamptons. It's July. I can have a normal life—at least for three weeks. There's a phone in the house, but no Internet and no satellite connection for my cell.

But, two days into my vacation, a real-estate colleague manages to get hold of me to ask about a listing I once had. It's everything he needs, he tells me. It's off the market, I tell him.

"Ask if there's any price at which they'd sell," he responds.

I phone them. They'd sell for $11 million, they tell me. Since they bought it at $1.2 million, they feel that this is a reasonable appreciation.

No chance in hell, I think. But my colleague shows the house, and the customer loves it and agrees to their price of $11 million.

All this in four or five phone calls. I make an announcement at dinner that night that I am going to be rich. We toast to me. We toast to Deer Isle and taking time off. *This is my lucky island*, I think. I spend the rest of the time on the beach, drinking good wine and buying lobster dinners for everyone.

When I return home, I find that a closing has been set two weeks hence and that the buyer is paying all cash. The owners move their furniture out, have the house painted, look at other houses to buy, and approve the contracts their lawyer has drawn up. Everything is simple and straightforward. I've been in the business for twenty years and finally, finally, all the hard work has paid off, and my ship has come in.

Two weeks come and go. The buyer texts my colleague that he is caught in Greece on a ship in the middle of a mistral and can't get to the mainland. A week later, he sends a message that his wife has been in a car crash in Milan. Another week goes by and his wife has come down with tuberculosis. The sellers get suspicious and remind me that the buyer didn't look rich. I remind them that it's the Hamptons.

But at the end of the month, the buyer e-mails that Homeland Security is holding up his money. The sellers make arrangements to have their furniture put back in the house. They're not talking to me, and their lawyer is demanding payment for the contract he wrote up in such a hurry.

At the end of September, the guy e-mails that his money has finally been released from Homeland Security, and he'll be in New York to sign the contract and close the deal in a week. The sellers are hesitant to move their furniture out a second time, and they put the mover on hold.

A week goes by, and nothing happens; we can't reach the buyer. At the end of September, he materializes. He is in New York and driving out. Three hours later he e-mails that his car has broken down on the Long Island Expressway and that he'll messenger the money over on Monday.

The sellers say they're closing up the house and leaving for Paris. I cancel my trip to Morocco. I cancel the large order I placed with J. Jill. I make an appointment to have my car serviced earlier than I'd intended. I stop eating out.

But the buyer re-emerges. "I'm coming in October to close and take over the house," he says. The sellers laugh when I call them to tell them this, but I think I hear a bit of wouldn't-it-have-been-wonderful wistfulness, even though there seems no earthly chance.

A year goes by. The buyer has yet to disappear. We receive periodic e-mails from him saying he's on his way. The sellers are perfectly happy with their house and glad now that it didn't sell. I make no plans for the year except to return to Maine, where I will rent a house—my only stipulation being that it must come without a phone.

Two years later, we finally track the "buyer" down. He is a vagrant, living in a homeless shelter in the Bronx. He had found a cell phone whose phone plan allowed for unlimited calls and texting.

"Boy, I envy you; you show a couple of houses, you get a huge commission. What a racket!"

Epilogue

When we started out in real estate in the nineteen eighties, "The Hamptons" weren't The Hamptons," they were just a string of small villages- Amagansett, East Hampton, Wainscott, Sagaponack, Bridgehampton, Water Mill, and Southampton. Back then, no one *ever* said they were looking for a house in "East" or "Bridge." The main industries then were fishing and farming. There were small family-owned and run stores. There were artists and writers, painting and writing and of course, drinking. The very wealthy had been out here for a century, but they kept a low profile. There were real-estate offices, but not many, and the people who came out then were mainly looking to rent for the summer. The beach was the main draw. The houses were nice and simple, furnished with yard-sale finds; maybe the landlord slapped a fresh coat of paint on the house before the season. Tenants would come back from the beach, sweep out the sand, and light the charcoal grill. They brought their own sheets and towels too. When they did look to buy, it was for a house to use from Memorial Day through Labor Day, after which they'd drain the pipes, close the house up until spring, and head back to their "real" houses and lives in the city.

Word got out, and things changed. The more people who came out, the more amenities they wanted. They wanted a house that looked like the ones in *Architectural Digest*. Owners got the idea, spruced up their homes, and charged a lot more money. The renters became buyers, the prices kept going up, and the sellers were making large profits. Houses ceased to be homes-Now they were investment properties. "South of the Highway" became important. Small business owners could no longer pay the sky-rocketing rents and high-end stores moved in. Farms were sold and subdivisions took their place. The fishermen couldn't make a living any longer, and only well-known artists and writers could afford to buy. The excesses of the 1990s and the early 2000s produced such large profits for home owners, they'd call a few months after buying to ask how much more could they get if they turned around and sold. Houses became just another item in their portfolios. They bought to impress their friends. Who's got the biggest kitchen with the most expensive appliances? The tennis courts, the media rooms, the wine cellars, the cigar rooms, and the gyms were of utmost importance.

All that has ended, at least for now; No one knows for how long. But maybe, just maybe, when this recession is over, things might return to what it used to be like at this end of Long Island. It's still a beautiful place; the light is magnificent, the beaches are gorgeous, the geese fly over in the fall, the swans still float on Town Pond, the windmills are still lit up at Christmastime, and who knows, maybe a house can once again be just a nice place to come to, and this, a nice place to live.